Principles Of Non-Euclidean Romance

Ela Bambust

ISBN 979-8-9873099-1-9

This book was professionally typeset by Cassidy Marble cassidy@marble.sh

A Confession

I am a criminal. English is my victim.
Should you look to point blame at those responsible, my accomplices
are these:

Noelle, a voice of madness in a sea of slightly more quiet mad-
ness.
Alexandra and Gwen, a hint of clarity on the cloudiest of days.
Juniper, a small cat.
Nicole, a touch of kindness in a world that sorely needs one.
They are still out there, wreaking havoc on language, and they can not
be stopped.

Thank you all.

TABLE OF CONTENTS

PROLOGUE

Space, as has been mentioned, is big. Mind-bogglingly so. You might think the collected five volumes of the *Hitchhiker's Guide To The Galaxy* are big, but that's peanuts compared to space. And that's not even getting into all the ways in which space is next to, on top of, or warping around in on itself in alternate realities.

Space has often been compared to the ocean, and that makes sense. The ocean is large, blue, cold, and human beings have a truly horrendous time trying to breathe any of it. Then there's the sense of wonder or, more sensibly, fear. There's a lot of dark out there, in the ocean/space, and it's tremendously easy to get lost in all that nothing.

But then there's the differences. In the ocean, lighter things go up, heavy things go down, and tasty things that wriggle a lot tend to go down a lot faster. In space, "up" is a very nebulous concept, and weight is only important when you bump into something.

What most people don't realize, however, is that space and the ocean are a lot more similar than most people think. For one thing, did you know that you can sail in space? Solar sails catch something called solar winds, and it allows you to travel at relatively high speeds. The other important thing that space and the ocean have in common is that there are very large, hungry creatures that swim around in them that eat people who don't believe in them.

There are things that don't reflect light, swimming from star to star, devouring planets and scaring the bejeezus out of turn-of-the-century racist authors. These things are older than most planets, and might even be older than time itself, although the only ones who would know are those things themselves, and they aren't likely to talk about these matters unless they've had a *lot* to drink.

They live in Space. They also live in the space, not only between planets and suns but the space between *worlds*. The space between choices, between realities. What old science-fiction authors would refer to as 'dimensions.'

Imagine, if you'll indulge me for a moment,

one of those things. Large. Impossibly so. Eyes the size of moons, glistening softly in the infinite dark between everything out there, blinking in what appears to be all-knowing indifference. Imagine it currently swimming between Saturn and Jupiter, avoiding Uranus because of the obvious joke.

You can see its shadow darkening Saturn's rings, giving you a kind of vague idea of its shape. It's not a very good shape. It's a shape that has a lot of tentacles and teeth in all the wrong places. If you tilt your head sideways, it looks a little bit like a very angry melting octopus. If you tilt your head the other way around, it might remind you of an angry scribble that an eight-year-old might draw in the margins of their math homework.

It's also swimming in a big circle, and that circle isn't around the sun. It doesn't really care for the sun. The sun can't hurt it (much) but it also can't really hurt the sun without having a toothache for several weeks afterwards. Stars aren't really worth the effort for a planet-devouring entity. However, the solar system has other things in it.

You can probably see where I'm going with this. Of all the small spheres orbiting the sun, the third one tends to be the most talked about. It's blue, and it's the only one — for now — where someone is able to watch videos of cats falling asleep, and that's a recent development. When drawing a map of the solar system, this is the one we draw a little smiling face on with the note "Here Be People."

This unspeakable, unknowable, impossible monstrous thing that could engulf the Earth in seconds is currently circling that little blue ball. I know what you're thinking to yourself. "Either this thing is going to eat the whole world, in which case this is going to be a very short story, or there's going to be some kind of brilliant subversion and I'm going to go 'heh' when I read it."

Well… yes. You see, this creature has been swimming through the universe since the dawn of time. It has seen civilizations rise and fall. Star-empires grow and crumble. Life and death on scales unimaginable to the likes of us, barely a fleck of dust in one of its eyes. And there, in those eyes, lies a knowledge that would drive even the strongest wills mad:

Space is boring. It's unimaginably boring. It's pretty, sure, with all the colors and the planets and stuff. But after you've spent an aeon or three with nothing but space, you too will wish you had a pillow half an astronomical unit wide to scream into. Space doesn't have a lot in it that isn't planets, and when you're bigger than one, there's spectacularly little to do in it.

I'll be referring to this creature as Sammaël for no reason you should concern yourself with right now. Just accept that that makes it easier to talk about something in a way that doesn't feel so objectively distant. Sammaël is bored. Unimaginably bored.

Once upon a time, Sammaël was just another impossible eldritch being, and those are a dime a dozen. "The monstrosities from beyond the stars", we've all seen them. But then its unknowable, vast intellect picked something up.

A radio signal. It was a song, and it was

coming from a small blue planet circling a little star on the Orion-Cygnus arm. Sammaël, for the first time in its life, experienced something new. Curiosity. Sure, it had seen *life* before, but for some reason that life had never really meant much to it, in the same way that ants don't mean much to mountains.

But that one song had lodged itself into its unfathomably large mind. It kept playing itself, back and forth, and so, finally, the creature had swam impossibly large distances, to come look at the planet itself. To see what it is like on that little blue ball in all possible realities, and to see if there are any other fun songs to pick up on in any of them.

Here it is now, observing the little planet, observing the little creatures on it, and wondering for the first time in its unimaginably long lifespan how it is going to get down there. Sammaël quietly hums the song to itself, making the rings around Saturn vibrate in ways that will confuse scientists for years to come. It's trying to think of a way to set foot on Earth, and it's slowly hatching a plan.

Sammaël's corporeal shape has always been more of a rough concept than something explicitly defined. Its outside seems to constantly shift and change, like a cloud in a storm, and now it is considering maybe trying something different. After all, its intellect is vaster than any ocean on any world, and its mind can observe all realities at once, but it is *too* detached. It perceives, it is starting to understand, but it does not see.

So, as it lazily swims past Jupiter, causing a shadow to fall across it that terrifies several school children on a field-trip to an observatory, it molds something. Not a body, no. Bodies come later. That's just the physical. Right now it is working on something much more important: a mind that might fit inside of a body.

It's hard work, and not particularly pleasant. Sammaël is having a rough time trying to find and create a version of itself that wouldn't immediately collapse if it was put into a body as small as a human's. Its memories aren't all that important, and take up hardly any space at all. While it might have a perfect memory that goes all the way back to the beginning of the universe, there isn't a lot *to* that memory. It's mostly Sammaël swimming and eating and, occasionally, driving someone utterly mad with its horrible visage.

The biggest issue is its perspective. It's very hard to fit the perception of a brain the size of a planet into one that is no larger than a grain of sand by comparison. So Sammaël takes its time making its way towards Earth, and comes to a few realizations. The first is that maybe it doesn't have to at all. Maybe it can just stay connected to the larger whole, like dipping a sentient little toe into a pool.

The mind it creates is like a miniature version of itself that is still a part of the large whole. Everything it thinks, Sammaël also perceives. Everything it feels, Sammaël will feel. Sammaël is quite proud of this solution.

The second realisation is that it has no idea what body to take. It looks down at the planet and then looks a little closer. It's full of people, all of them in different little colours and sizes and shapes. Barely any two are the same. It spins up, in a mind that can make thought into reality, a body that is the perfect average. It looks like a lot of nothing, like mixing every shade of paint before trying to make a rainbow.

So it tries making a few different ones. Taking some limbs from one here, some internal plumbing from another, with the head of a last one. It doesn't work. It looks like a broken doll.

This is vexing. Something is wrong. Sammaël is confused. After all, it's created life before, in some backwater dimension, slamming proteins together until something invents the hamburger, but this is different. It's not trying to create life from scratch, it's trying to create a *person*. And people are much more than just "life", and Sammaël is having trouble understanding that.

So, Sammaël feels, if it is not capable of creating the perfect vessel yet, that is due to a lack of information. This information is probably most easily gathered through experience. So, it needs a human body to experience what a human body is really like in order to create a human body so that it can experience... Oh dear.

It observes a little bit more, like someone trying to go to sleep but deciding to have one last guilty little look at social media, and it notices something. A lot of people don't use their bodies anymore. At some point, they stop moving, the light upstairs goes out, and the body just sort of starts to decompose without the mind telling it not to.

This all seems very wasteful, Sammaël appears to think with its cosmic intellect. Have they considered *not* doing that? Well, it reasons, there is only one way to find *that* out, and that is to ask them. And it can ask them if it has a body.

And, it seems, there are a lot of bodies no-one is using anymore. Now, it doesn't want to use one of the ones near the ends of its lifecycle, that would greatly limit its ability to experience things. It also doesn't want one that's been "out of commission" for too long, for the same reason.

So it looks around for some bodies that might not be in use. Something that's still fairly new, but recently vacated. There might be a little bit of residual damage, but that can be fixed when it moves in.

There.

It's found something. A body that has recently stopped moving, the mind now gone. Sammaël knows where minds go when they die, but it isn't telling. Who would it tell, after all, and why? So it takes its little sculpted mini-Sammaël, a version of its mind that is capable of feeling and thinking on its own and, much more importantly, capable of listening to Jammin' Tunes. Sammaël is *so* ready to experience things.

In an alleyway on Earth, Abraham 'Abe' Douglas died. Not in any dignified way either. His ever-so-slightly-drunk ex-future-brother-in-law, Morris, was still rubbing his hand when it dawned on him that the other man wasn't moving anymore, and that his head was resting against the wall in a very uncomfortable angle.

"Abe?" Morris asked. "Abe, you had *better* not be fucking with me right now." He swore to himself as he leaned in close and checked Abe's eyes. There was no response. "Fuck", he said.

That didn't quite do it. "Fuck fuck fuck fuck fuck fuck fuck."

Morris was in the middle of a major dilemma, exacerbated by the four beers he'd had the last fifteen minutes. If he ran now, it would probably look like Abe just slipped on a bottle in an alley and hit his head. It would be *entirely* in character for the bastard, after all. But then his sister would find out by cop, and that was pretty awful too. So what, then? Tell her he killed the guy she'd been planning to marry, once? Morris looked down at the body. "You prick", he said. "You probably did this on purpose, didn't you?" He wanted to add something else, something glib, while processing the fact that he hit someone so hard he'd died. Sure, there were extenuating circumstances and Abe probably deserved it, but Morris wasn't exactly killer material. He opened his mouth, just as Abe Douglas' corpse jumped upright.

Well, that wasn't quite right. It didn't jump. It went from horizontal to vertical without going through all the usual steps in between. Morris frowned. That wasn't right. Then Abe's neck straightened itself with the horrifying sound of someone sitting on a glass ornament, and his lifeless eyes stopped being lifeless. They rolled around in Abe's head like two loose marbles until they finally stopped on Morris. "Did what?" Abe said.

Morris screamed. Abe screamed too, took a step back onto a bottle and slipped. Falling backwards, he cracked his skull against the wall, and stopped moving.

Chapter 1

MADE YOU PERFECT, BABE

Sammaël has just died, which it finds mildly annoying. Eldritch entities, born in the blackness between stars before those pinpricks even came into being, are not used to being dead*, but Sammaël is learning quite rapidly. The meat-brain it has just stuffed a chunk of itself into seems to have rapidly experienced deceleration and that caused the whole thing to stop for some reason.

Now the rest of it gently circles the moon for a bit, considering what to do next. It could go *down* there. It might take the species a couple of centuries to rebuild, but that seems like a small price to pay. On the other hand, it *has* spent time crafting this identity, and finding a good body to put it in. It seems, to Sammaël, a little bit of a wasted effort if it was to try and find a different one.

---

*Nor are they used to being annoyed. Default states include "malevolence" and "indifference."

So, Sammaël does the most logical thing, and takes a diagonal step through time. Why this step is diagonal instead of sideways or backwards, for example, is a question only Sammaël can answer. While it has generally moved through time linearly, it doesn't strictly speaking have to. It just hasn't seen any reason not to. Until now.

Sammaël steps diagonally through time. Just a few seconds. What, the eldritch abomination wonders to itself, is the worst that could happen? The brain that has just been scrambled is now not. Abe Douglas has just died. Again. So, this time, instead of fixing Abe's neck completely, Sammaël just aligns things a little bit. Just enough for its mind to exist inside that fragile little brain. There.

It resists the urge to immediately jump upright again, and instead lets the version of itself it has just stuffed inside of a human body take full control. With a bit of apprehension, it lets go and... Immediately, the identity blips away from Sammaël's perception. Right. Abe's body is still unconscious.

Sammaël crosses its arms, leans its massive

consciousness on top of the moon, and frowns, staring down at the earth. Nothing to do now, but wait.

"Yes, I'm— No, I'm telling you I *am* a relative."

"Fwizl blillip"

"I'm his fiancee."

"Fz dvvnt lippit sip—"

"We're going through a rough patch. Just let me talk to him. Please."

"Wivvy wip."

"Thank you."

Only one of the two voices was comprehensible. It was a pretty good voice, the kind of voice that promised things Sammaël didn't quite know how to place yet, like mint tea and sunlit parks and, right now, possibly a smack around the ear and a lawsuit.

The other voice was indignant. It was a voice that sounded like ashtrays and unpaid overtime. More importantly, it was muffled. Sammaël figured it was possible that was due to its brain being scrambled more than anything, though. It was trying to think, which was harder than it had previously thought. Up until recently, it had been an entity to which the concept of a continent was a curiosity, in the same way a person goes "Oh, really? Interesting!" when someone has told them for the first time what a quark is.

Now, Sammaël was trying to find the words for what it was experiencing. There was so much. Sounds, which it knew was language. Abe's brain was full of language, so it understood a good chunk of it. Smells, which were... unpleasant. It smelled like the side of a star, and Sammaël had gone through some real gastrointestinal issues last time it had eaten one of those. Touch. Something weighing down on it.

However, there was something much more pressing, and much more present. It was a wholly new sensation, a fascinating one that it had no way to relate to, no way to place it. The sensation bounced around its skull, and was refusing to be ignored. Sammaël took a hard, long look at it, and decided to give it a name. And, in order to put some power behind that name, it decided to speak it, because names are Important.

"I have a headache", Sammaël said.

"He's awake", the indignant voice said, now audible. "Sir, please don't try to speak or sit up", the voice continued with calculated disinterest. "You're in the hospital, do you remember anything?"

Sammaël opened its eyes. For the first time in its life, it only had two. And they weren't even focusing properly. "I have a headache", it repeated, hoping this would answer any questions the person had for Abe Douglas. Sammaël had the distinct impression that "Yes, everything", would not be taken well. Humans were, as it had discovered, incredibly fragile.

"I understand that, sir", the ashtray voice continued, "but I'm going to have to ask you to answer the question."

"Jesus Christ", the sunlight voice said.

Sammaël thought for a moment. What would the voice find acceptable? Humans experienced time as a linear line of events, so perhaps, going backwards was the answer. "It was dark. I was asleep", it said.

The person the ashtray voice was attached to rolled their eyes. "Before that, sir."

This line of questioning didn't make a lot of sense to Sammaël. It had demonstrated that it was able to conceptualize linear progression of time, and memory of that progression. Wasn't that the most important part? Regardless, it obliged. "An alleyway. Another person was present."

"Do you remember who was there?"

"His name is Morris Guthrie. He is thirty-one years old. He lives on the corner of Park and Fifth", Sammaël said. It had no idea what any of this information meant, but Abe had known it so it did too. "He is the brother of the woman Abraham Douglas was recently engaged to."

"And that's you", the person said. Sammaël frowned. That was an extremely vague statement. Were they referring to Morris, to the person Abraham Douglas had been engaged to, or to Abraham Douglas? It thought it best to answer with a — mostly — factually correct statement.

"I am Abraham 'Abe' Douglas", it said.

"He seems fine", ashtray voice said to sunshine voice. "Either you take him with you, or you give me his insurance information."

Sunshine voice stepped closer, and Sammaël recognized her. "Sierra", it said, reflexively, and then took a moment to reflect on that reflex. It had spoken without intending to. That was a new sensation. Sammaël had never done anything without intending to.

"Yes", Sierra said. "Get up." Sammaël blinked a few times, then did as it was told, sitting upright. Moving a body around was remarkably easy, although disorienting. If it had possessed the right experiences and vocabulary, it might have compared itself to someone or something wearing an ill-fitting suit[†]. "Morris told me what happened", Sierra said. "Can't say you didn't have it coming, Abe."

Sammaël sifted through Abraham's memories again, searching for context. There was a lot of context. Five years of it, and the human

---

[†]Like a plastic glove filled with baked beans in tomato sauce.

brain, it seemed, was not good at holding a lot of complex thoughts at once. Trying to think of all of it at once was not working. So, Sammaël was once again forced to approach these memories in order of reverse chronology.

"The alcohol", Sammaël said as Sierra helped it up. Hitting the floor made the headache instantly worse. Sierra shook her head.

"No, you ass, not the alcohol. Well, okay, partly the alcohol, but you can't just pretend like you didn't *skip on my fucking wedding day.*" Her look was one of abject fury. "You're lucky Morris didn't kill you." She led it out of the room. Sammaël followed dutifully, still trying to get used to the body. It walked slowly, since big steps seemed to make the throbbing worse.

"Yes", Sammaël said dryly. "Lucky."

"What were you even *thinking?* Like, not even about the wedding! Drinking? In Morris' watering hole? What did you think was going to happen?" Sammaël stopped for a moment. Memories were easy, if it knew what it was looking for. It was simply a matter of sorting through data. Meaning was harder. Who someone was in relation to itself. What the correct way to respond to a question was. But understanding what Abraham had been thinking? Why he had made the choices and decisions he'd made? That was beyond it.

"I... do not know", it said truthfully. "I am sure it seemed like a good idea at the time."

"You must've hit your head pretty hard", Sierra said. "It's not like you to be so introspective." They reached the doors and sunlight, real sunlight this time, pierced Sammaël's eyes. It squinted. "Take it easy." Seeping through the apparently well-deserved anger, there was a hint of concern in her voice. When they got to her car, Sierra stopped and leaned against it. "Look, Abe. I don't know what's going on with you. But if this is some kind of cry for help..."

"I could use help", Sammaël said. The relationship between Abe and Sierra had clearly been strained, but there appeared to be enough of a connection there for her to help it figure some things out. While experiencing new things like

22

music was its eventual goal, it would be well served to be around longer. And that would require assistance.

"Yeah, no shit", Sierra said. "Get in the fucking car, Abe."

Sammaël did as it was told and sat down. It felt a strange impulse, to move its arms a certain way. Searching through Abraham's memories, there was a ritual that was done every time. Sammaël fastened its seatbelt.

"Jesus, you're really not alright, are you?" Sierra said, her brow furrowed. "Yeah, I'm not dropping you off at your place, you're going to kill yourself like that."

"I do not intend to", Sammaël said. The look Sierra gave him was one of disbelief, but she didn't say anything. Oh well, that just gave him more room to figure out where to go from here. He wanted to do well enough to exist on this little planet for a while. Experience plenty of things. Who even knew how many of those songs there were on this planet? Four? Five? It looked forward to listening to them all several times.

"Sierra", it said.

"Abe."

"I am having some difficulty in trying to know or understand what to say", it said. Sierra looked at him for a moment but didn't say anything, then started the car and drove out of the parking lot. "I do not know what to do in certain situations, and it seems you harbor me, Abraham Douglas, ill will." Sierra scoffed. "And with reason. Actions I, Abraham Douglas have taken, have impacted you severely and negatively. What actions could I take that would impact you positively, and how?"

"Wh— Just like that?" The only reason Sierra wasn't staring at it was because she was clearly trying to keep an eye on the road. "You can't be fucking serious."

"I am serious", Sammaël said.

"I — Alright. Fine. Great. Fine. Okay, let's start with the first thing then: I'd like a *fucking* apology, Abe." She shot him another withering glance, this time out of the corner of her eye. "If you even know what you're apologizing for."

Sammaël looked back. This was going to take

a while. Abe had done a great many things that had screwed Sierra over, and he hadn't felt guilty about a single one of them. But he'd known they were awful all the same. But there was one that stood out.

"I apologize for ruining your wedding. For leaving you standing at the altar. For becoming inebriated and embarrassing you in front of people who mean a great deal to you. For causing you deep and possibly long-lasting emotional pain, in general and more specifically on a day that, as I understand it, is more important to you than almost any other."

"Why did you do it?"

"Because Abraham Douglas is a coward."

"Because you're a coward?"

"No."

"What does that mean?"

"I am not a coward."

"But you're—"

"I am not Abraham Douglas."

Chapter 2

TRY TO MAKE SOME SENSE OF IT ALL

"What the *fuck* does that mean, Abe? If you're trying to tell me that you're turning over a new leaf just because you saw god or something—"

"I mean to say that Abraham Douglas died in an alley approximately..." It looked at the car's clock. "Five hours ago. I'm just here in his place."

"That's not..." Sierra rubbed her face. "I swear to god..."

"That isn't necessary", Sammaël said. "It is within the realm of the reasonable for you to be suspicious of any radical changes in the behavior of someone you know. It seems Abraham was duplicitous, at times?"

"Yeah, 'Abe was duplicitous', all right. Pretending you're not him doesn't exactly fill me with confidence either." She parked the car and looked at the person sitting next to her with the skepticism one usually reserves for food found in the back of the fridge.* Her grip on the steering wheel tightened enough for her knuckles to go white. "So you're not Abe. Who are you, then? And this had better not be you trying some new shit."

"I have had many names before", it said, then looked at her for a moment. "I suspect that this answer is insufficient." Sierra just scoffed in response. "I am as old as time itself, and have seen what exists beyond the stars. I've swallowed stars whole, and have seen the rise and fall of civilizations so large and ancient they would make your entire species seem like a fleck of dust in a blizzard." It cocked its head. "You may call me Sammaël."

"This is the second worst attempt at pretending you're having a psychotic break I've seen out of you yet, Abe. You can do better than that." Sierra sighed, shook her head and opened her door. "Look, if you're going to stick to that story

---

*The carton of milk that doesn't have cultures so much as it has civilizations.

for a while, 'Sammaël', you're coming upstairs with me, and you're making yourself useful."

"If that pleases you", Sammaël said, but made no motions to open the door yet. "Can I listen to music?" Sierra gave him a look of utter confusion, then rubbed the bridge of her nose.

"Yes. Yes, you can listen to music." She slammed the door shut, and finally Sammaël stepped out of the car too. "Come on." Sammaël followed dutifully as she led it up the steps to the apartment, and up to the third floor. The apartment was pretty small. Sammaël found, in Abraham Douglas' memories, some explanations and reasons. A hasty break-up, a lease signed as quickly as possible, for her to get away from *him*. It looked around. Disregarding some boxes in a corner, the room was pretty well-furnished. The living room, kitchen and dining room were all a single space, but with enough room to not feel claustrophobic.[†]

_____

[†]Claustrophobia can be a problem when you're used to wearing nebulae as a scarf.

Once inside, she tossed her purse and jacket onto the sofa. "Alright, suppose I humor you for a moment, and you're some ancient star-thing, what can you do?" She shoved her hands in her pockets and leaned against her kitchen counter. "Any magic tricks? Maybe you can show me 'your true form' or something?"

"I could", Sammaël said, standing in the middle of the room with its arms by its side, "but it would likely drive you mad. My full form exists in more dimensions than most sapient minds are capable of conceptualizing. And it's currently on the far side of the moon; I'm a construct thereof. Can I listen to music?"

"I... Yes", Sierra said, and turned the radio on. "Listen... I don't know what's going on with you. You're clearly going through something. So you're going to prove to me that this isn't just you trying another scam or whatever. So here's what we're going to do. I've taken the day off from work to come pick *your* sorry ass up from the hospital, so a couple of things: One, you're going to call insurance and get that taken care of. Two, you're going to pay back the money you've taken from my wallet when you thought I wasn't looking — I wrote it all down, don't worry. You can do it in installments. Three, you're going to call my parents, right here, in front of me, on speaker, and you're apologizing to them. Are you *crying?*"

"Yes", Sammaël said. "It's the music. It... stirs something inside me."

"Nobody cries listening to the Vengaboys!"

"It seems", it said, wiping the tears out of its eyes, "that I do. And your demands seem reasonable. Would you prefer I introduce myself as Abraham Douglas when I speak to your parents?"

"I... Yes. Drop the 'Douglas." She spun around and started the electric kettle, and grabbed a box of tea bags from the cupboard. "Still take coffee?"

"I don't know", Sammaël said. "I have never experienced liquid food myself."

"Well, *'Abe'* was addicted to the stuff. Since I'm making tea, and you're not Abe, you might as well have a cup of tea then, right?" She took out two cups. It pretended not to notice her looking at it out of the corner of her eye.

"That would be amenable. I'll take what-ever you think is appropriate." It turned around the room a few times. "Do you have a phone I could use? I believe Abraham Douglas' phone is broken."

"Yeah, of course it is. Let's start with my parents", Sierra said sweetly, putting her phone on the counter, then putting it on speaker. She poured two cups of tea as the dial tone bounced off the walls of the apartment. Sammaël was content to stand in front of it patiently, though it was slightly disappointed to see her turning the radio down.

"Hello?" a voice on the other side said. Abra-ham's memory revealed it to be Sierra's mother. *"Sierra? Hello, is that you? Is everything okay?"*

"Yeah", Sierra said, "hi, Mom. No, every-thing's fine. I'm just calling because... well, you'll never *believe* who I ran into today. And he has something to say to you! Is Dad there? This is for him, too."

"Yes, of course, sweetie. Dan! Come here for a

second!" There was an unintelligible second voice in the distance that gave Sammaël the distinct impression of a small animal trapped in a tin can. It kept that observation to itself. *"He's here. Well, who is it, dear?"*

"Hello", Sammaël said. "This is Abraham." It looked at Sierra, who raised her eyebrows. "Abe", it added.

"What do you want?" the other voice on the line growled. Sierra's father. He sounded upset, which Sammaël couldn't blame him for. *"If you're looking for help with something—"*

Sierra interrupted him. "No, he just wants to say something, Dad. You'll want to hear him out." She stepped back, one hand on her hip, and gestured at the phone. "All yours", she said quietly.

"I am calling to apologize to you. What... I did to your daughter, both in the recent past and throughout my relationship with her, was not acceptable. I understand that this also reflects negatively on you as parents, and has, obviously, hurt you as well as hurt her."

32

"What the fuck are you talking about, Douglas? If you're looking for forgiveness, you're not getting it here."

"I'm not looking for forgiveness, Mister Guthrie", Sammaël said, looking directly at Sierra. "It is my honest and sincere belief that, while an apology here will not solve any problems created by past actions, it is nonetheless necessary and something you — all of you — have a right to."

The other side of the line was quiet for a while. *"I appreciate your candor. Now, never call here again and put my daughter back on the phone. If I ever see you I'll kick y—"* There was some noise as Mrs Guthrie wrested the phone out of Mr Guthrie's hand.

"Yes, Mister Guthrie. The best to you and your wife." It stepped back and looked expectantly at Sierra, who looked genuinely surprised. She stepped forward and picked up the phone.

"Yeah. No, yeah, that was really him. I know. No, don't worry, I won't." She grabbed one of the cups and handed it to Sammaël, then waved it away.

It slowly walked around the room, trying
to stay within range of the radio well enough
to keep listening. Abe's memories recognized
the song currently playing, but to Sammaël, the
experience was still new. And Bonnie Tyler's
Holding Out For A Hero was quickly making it
feel overwhelmed, which was a completely new
experience on its own.

Sammaël stepped over to the sofa and sat
down. It briefly closed its eyes to listen to the
music, but found it actually easier to keep them
open. If its eyes were closed, there was *only* the
music, and that was just... too much. It needed
some reality to dilute the music, or it risked
becoming emotional again.

In front of it was a giant television. Abraham's
memories told it that Sierra had taken it in the
breakup, but that was... background information.
Unimportant. What was interesting to Sammaël
at that exact moment was the television's black, re-
flective surface. For the first time, it saw Abraham
Douglas' face. It was not impressed.

Sammaël cocked its head. The figure in the

reflection did too. Abraham Douglas had been cultivating the feel, if not the exact look, of a used car salesman. Hair slicked back. Bags under his eyes. His handlebar mustache didn't so much stop as it tapered off in the vague direction of his sideburns, and now that it was on Sammaël's face, it was very much no longer desired.

It ran its fingers across its face, feeling the tough bristles of its facial hair against the palm of its hand. The feeling was uncomfortable. It stood up and turned around. "Sierra." She looked up from her phone just as she hung up.

"What?"

"Do you have shaving supplies I might use? This facial hair makes me uncomfortable." Sierra stared at him for a couple of seconds. Her mouth fell open.

"All right", she said, standing up. "Either you're fucking with me, or you're *genuinely really serious* about being someone else, because Abe would never shave off that rat on his upper lip. I've got a trimmer in my bathroom, and I've got to see this."

Several minutes later, Sammaël was looking into the bathroom mirror, shaving off the offending facial hair. It fell in wads into the sink. Sierra stood in the door behind him, arms crossed and leaning against the door frame. The little radio was on the toilet, currently blaring *Killer Queen*, Freddie Mercury giving it his all.

"No fucking way", Sierra said. "I thought you'd chicken out or just... trim the sides. But you're really just... getting rid of all of it, huh?"

"It's physically unpleasant", Sammaël said. "Abraham found it amenable — though I can't say *why* — but I will not." It looked at Sierra. "Should have found myself a body like yours."

Sierra raised an eyebrow like that. "What the fuck is that supposed to mean?"

"I mean to say that the form you are in has fewer anatomical quirks that keep it from enjoying music the way this one does. The facial hair, for example, is... distracting. It feels wrong, and I do not know why Abraham put up with it."

"You're... really different, aren't you?"

"I would hope so", Sammaël said. "Abraham

36

Douglas seems like he was a thoroughly unpleasant individual who got in his own way as much as he did other people. If I'm to... be here a while, I would like to find a way to undo some of that damage." It didn't mention that it wished to do so because *not* doing so would mean people getting into the way of it listening to music.

"Well... As long as none of this manages to blow up in your face in a way that fucks me over... Abe owes me. Or... owed me, I guess. So I'm going to — tentatively — be around to observe what you do next."

Sammaël washed the hair down the drain, put the trimmer aside, then turned around. It ran a hand across its jaw. "This is still too rough. Deeply unpleasant. Do you have a razor?" For the first time in her life, Sierra guffawed.

Chapter 3

Fascinations Galore

"You know", Sierra said with her hands on her hips, "I'm still trying to find a crack in your story." Sammaël looked at her in the mirror as it cleaned off its face with the towel, ran a hand over its jaw, and was reasonably satisfied with the results. It wasn't *perfect*, but it wasn't nearly as unpleasant to the touch as it had been. "But you haven't let up on the weird speech patterns once, I haven't seen you crack that annoying grin once, and you don't even stand like he — like *you* — used to."

"He slouched", Sammaël said. "It was causing kyphosis. This would have meant severe distress in five to ten years. With proper posture and exercise, this should be staved off." It stood upright and moved its neck experimentally, happy with the results.

"Exercise?" Sierra shook her head and head to her fridge. "God, I need a drink, this can't be real." She seemed to change her mind and poured herself another cup of tea instead. "Alright, what else can you do to prove it, 'Sammaël'?" She sipped her cup as Sammaël retrieved its own cup. "Any proof that you are who you say you are? *What* you say you are?"

"I can not show you my true form, Sierra", it said, "as I explained, it would cause you extreme mental harm." It held up a hand as she rolled her eyes in response. "That does not mean I do not have a large measure of control over this reality, though I am severely limited in this form." It cocked its head and went over its options.

Sammaël tried to think the way it always had, running billions of concepts through its head. It wanted to give a good example. Its brain, however, didn't.* Its brain managed two or three options instead. This was frustrating for a number of reasons, but the weaknesses of the flesh had been an expected side-effect of its little project. At the end of the day, Sammaël was here to experience

---

*If it had, much like trying to squeeze a swimming pool into a water balloon, it would have exploded quite spectacularly.

music first-hand, in a body that was good at experiencing music.

But that meant that it was having trouble conceptualizing the optimal way to convince Sierra that Sammaël was itself. A physical transformation could help, but that would come, again, with the risk of killing Sierra or possibly unraveling reality itself. Reality isn't very stable to begin with, after all.

"How about something small?" Sierra offered. "If reality is at your whim or whatever, just change your appearance. Or make something float. Should be easy, right?"

Sammaël observed her for a moment. "I worry about the structure of the universe if I distort it too much", it said. "A localized disruption of gravity, for example, could cause a disruption on a quantum scale that could cascade into a full collapse of this planet's gravitational field. But appearance..."

Sierra crossed her arms skeptically and raised an eyebrow. "What?"

It waited for a moment, and then had an idea

40

looking out the window. "Perhaps I can show you without showing." It turned to face her. "Please look into my eyes, Sierra." She did as it asked her, with a reluctant sigh, and saw the universe.

Messing with the nature of reality, Sammaël knew, was a sketchy proposition at best. It knew, because it did so all the time, but only on a scale that was either unimaginably small or unimaginably large. Before the first stars had come into being, Sammaël had already ripped several holes in spacetime. While not strictly speaking the end of the universe, it had been annoying to deal with. On a planet like this, it would probably cause untold destruction, not to mention the end of music.

But light? Light was *easy*. Light could be bounced around and bent like a toy. It was a little bit like time, in that way, even though Sammaël found both to be a little bit more difficult to wrap its head around while in this frail little body. A little, however, was not enough. Not enough to stop it from showing Sierra how it saw the universe reflected in eyes as deep and as black as the void between billions and billions of stars.

Realization dawned on Sierra as she stared into the Abyss and realized it was not only staring back but was wearing her ex-boyfriend's face. "Oh", she said as tears ran down her eyes, most of her world-view shattered in a single moment. Sammaël felt strangely... guilty? Guilt wasn't an experience it had much experience with. Guilt was not an emotion it had even felt before, and it was only tangentially aware of the fact that it even existed. "Oh", Sierra said again and crumpled to the ground.

Sammaël only barely managed to snatch her cup of tea out of the air. Some of the hot liquid spilled onto its hand, and its mouth made an involuntary hissing sound as the brain detected nerve damage. That was weird. But not important. It put the tea aside.

Then, instinctively, Sammaël crouched down next to Sierra. It didn't even know where that instinct had come from. It certainly hadn't been Abraham Douglas' first instinct. "I am sorry", it said. "That may have been a bit much, I am afraid. I hoped that if you saw the universe as I did..." Then what? It reflected on the action. Sierra would not, *could* not, understand. She was mortal. Finite. Fallible. Small. Fragile. But maybe she could believe?

"I-It's fine", Sierra said, wiping the tears from her face. "I'm fine. It's fine. I'm fine. I—"

"If you keep repeating yourself", Sammaël said, "I may have to call your statements into question." Sierra laughed and looked up at it. "I am sorry, I did not mean to be inappropriate. Do you need help standing?" It offered her a hand. She shook her head, then completely failed to stand up.

"Maybe", she said, eyeing the hand suspiciously. When it held up to scrutiny[†], she gingerly let it help her. When she was standing again — unsteadily, and leaning heavily against the couch — she wasn't facing Sammaël again. "Could you... turn that off?" she asked, waving at its eyes. "It's... hard."

[†] It didn't turn into a tentacle *at all*.

"I apologize again. Profusely." Its eyes resumed their regular shade again, whatever that was (it hadn't looked in the mirror long enough to take note of the eye color). "I did not mean to upset you, only to provide you with proof."

"It's fine. You're fine. I'm fine. Why wouldn't it be fine? You're some kind of space thing, an alien, and you just made me feel like I was floating in space and falling in every direction at the same time, just by looking me in the eyes. It's *fine*." She giggled a little and almost fell to the ground again. Sammaël immediately rushed forward to support her.

"I feel like you are having trouble navigating the information I have supplied you with, Sierra. Perhaps you wish to sit down?"

"Y-Yeah", she said, and let herself fall over the back of the couch and into the pillows. "You're right, this is so much better." She giggled again. "Holy shit. Holy *fuck*. This isn't real. This *can't* be real." Her head poked up over the back of the couch again. "You're really real?"

"I am", Sammaël said. "I am afraid that, as far

as I am aware, neither of the two of us is currently experiencing a hallucination, awake or otherwise."

"So what now? What do you want? You're an alien with superpowers that can change reality at a whim", she said, leaning her chin on her hands. "You came all this way to…"

"Listen to music", Sammaël said, pointing at the radio. "I like music."

"They don't have music in space?" Sierra said again with a giggle.

"Not like this", Sammaël said, cocking its head. "This is better."

"Well, guess I'm lucky then!" Her giggles slowly became more hysterical. "Oh my *god,* I made you apologize to my *parents!*"

"I thought it would help, considering the previous owner of this face", Sammaël said dryly. It offered Sierra the tea, hoping it would calm her down, and that she wouldn't spill any of it on herself. It could attest to the fact that it was still *quite* hot.

"Oh fuck, your *hand!*" she said and jumped over the back of the couch, grabbed the mug of tea and immediately put it down again, dragging Sammaël over to the tap. "This looks pretty badly burned. You didn't notice?"

"The damage is superficial", Sammaël said, "and this body will heal over time."

"Oh Christ, you really are an alien", Sierra said, and ran its hand under the tap. "It'll stop hurting faster and heal faster if you run it under cold water." She shook her head. "Men", she said. "Human or alien, you're all useless."

There was another reflex. And again, it wasn't Abe's. When Sammaël yanked its hand back, that was entirely its own instant reaction. "No", it said, realized what it had done, and sheepishly put its hand back under the tap. Sierra gave it a confused look. "I may currently inhabit the body of Abraham Douglas, but I am not him. My name is Sammaël, and I am not a man. To describe me as such is inaccurate and inefficient."

"I'm sorry", Sierra said with a bemused smile. "I didn't mean to offend you or anything."

"I am not..." Sammaël said. "I apologize, that was an overreaction." It let Sierra run water over its hand and it did feel the pain slowly subside. The sensation of pain was strange to Sammaël. On the surface it was a simple signal, but it was *distracting*.

"Will you be okay for a bit?" she asked. "I think I need to... uh... clear my head. I want to take a shower. There's a lot I need to think about and... so your name is really Sammaël?"

"It's a name I believe would make a degree of sense to you. Insofar as I can be said to have a name, that one can be said to be mine, even if it wasn't given to me", it said.

"Oh, so your species doesn't have names? Or do you not have a family."

"I do not have a species", Sammaël said matter-of-factly. "I simply am."

"That's kinda... sad, if you think about it", Sierra said, then shook her head. "Anyway, I'm going to take that shower. I need to... I gotta think." Sammaël observed her for a few seconds. All things considered, she was dealing with the knowledge that there was alien life and that that alien life was near omnipotent (most of the time) very well.

"That sounds like a good idea, Sierra", Sammaël said. "Would you mind if I listen to some more music?" It walked over to the radio eagerly. It was looking forward to examining what other music there was out there.

"Not at all. When I get out of the shower I'll show you my music library", Sierra said, then headed for the bathroom, stopping to look behind her. "It's nice to meet you." Sammaël, who was bent over the radio, paused and tried to return the smile. It was an uncomfortable and unfamiliar sensation.

"Thank you, Sierra", it said. "I suppose it is nice to meet you as well." After a few more seconds of the two of them looking at each other, Sierra finally started tearing herself away.

"I'm gonna... y'know..." She thumbed over her shoulder. Sammaël nodded and saw her take a step onto the towel that had fallen on the ground. It saw her slip, her one leg swinging way up in the air as she tried to find something to grab a hold of. The towel curtains were there, but they shot loose. Sammaël could only watch as the back of Sierra's head hit the edge of the bathtub with a wet crunch.

It stood up and walked over to her still body. "This is wrong", it said, then spooled and unspooled time. "I hate this part." Sammaël's head hit the brick wall. Again.

Chapter 4

CLOSE MY BODY NOW

"Yes, I'm— No, I'm telling you I *am* a relative."

"Whzt famiblzz?"

"I'm his fiancee."

"Fe dvvnt mentiffle a fia—"

"We're going through a rough patch. Just let me talk to him. Please."

"Vevvy welp."

"Thank you."

Sammaël blinked its eyes open. It was in the hospital bed again. It was good to hear Sierra's voice when it had been so horrifyingly interrupted before. The problem was that there were a lot of other things fighting for Sammaël's attention as well, just like the first time. The nauseating smell of the hospital. The background beeps and boops* and muttered voices. The burning brightness of the overhead fluorescent lights.

------

*No hospital is complete without a machine that goes 'ping'.

It decided not to speak of its headache. "I remember everything", it said to the ashtray woman, who seemed satisfied with its answer. "Abe Douglas. Engaged to Sierra Guthrie. My insurance information should be in order." It sat upright, which proved to be something of a mistake. Its head was pounding, but it didn't want to risk doing something about that. Its control of things like time and space was clearly more limited in this form.

"Jesus Christ", Sierra said, rubbing her face. "Of course money is the first thing you think of." Sammaël frowned for a moment, then remembered that Sierra experienced time completely linearly. She would not remember their previous conversation.

"Very well, Mister Douglas", the woman said. "How do you feel?"

"Well enough. I wish to leave." It swung its legs off the side of the bed, then winced. "I would appreciate something for the pain, however."

The woman shrugged and made for the door. "That should be covered. I'll be back in a moment."

"What the *fuck*, Abe?" Sierra said. "You get into a fight with Morris and manage to crack your own head open? You haven't caused enough sh—"

"I am not Abraham Douglas", Sammaël said. "That was a lie for her benefit. Lying is not pleasant." It stood up and walked over to Sierra. "We have had this conversation already, so I will try to make this as swift and painless as possible." Sierra frowned. "I am not Abraham Douglas. He died when his head hit that wall. I am a creature beyond your comprehension, inhabiting his body. I wish t—"

That was about as far as he got before Sierra's hand struck him square in the face with a *Thwack* that was as satisfying aurally as it was painful. The sound echoed through the room and bounced around Sammaël's head like a hyperreactive hamster in a tumble dryer.

"Ow", it said.

"How fucking *dare* you make light of this, Abe", Sierra said. "I don't care about your shit, I don't care about this weird... *thing* you're pulling, and I want this so fucking clear you can see yourself in the reflection, I don't care about *you*."

"Ah, yes", Sammaël said. "That requires clarification. Hrm." It paused for a moment. It realized that *this* Sierra had never received an apology, and therefore had no reason to treat it with kindness. On the other hand, there was the strange sense that it *had* already apologized. "Please look in my eyes, and know that I'm sorry about this."

Doing the trick again, letting its eyes be a reflection of the infinite cosmos that was its home, it looked Sierra in the eyes before she could protest or look away. It wasn't an elegant solution, but it was not in the mood to have a repeat of the same conversation again. Sierra's expression went from annoyance to shock, then abject terror.

She started stammering and fell to her knees, crawling backwards.

"Wh-wh-what— How— What—"

"Hrm", Sammaël said, "this is not the desired outcome. I am sorry, that was more abrupt than it should have been. Do not fear, I do not intend to harm you." Its words seemed to fall on deaf ears, reduced as she was to a gibbering mess. It took a step closer and kneeled down, next to her. "Sierra, you are not in danger. Please calm down."

She nodded, her eyes wide as she looked at it, reaching for her purse. Just then, the nurse walked in, and Sammaël looked over at her. She looked Sammaël in the eyes and screamed. It realized it should have probably turned the eyes back off. It looked back at Sierra just in time to see her shove a pocket knife — something it knew she had for protection but never used — into its neck.

"Ghrbl", Sammaël said, and died again.

"I'm a relative."

"Whzz fmzzly?"

"I'm... his fiancée."

"He divn't mentioffle a fia—"

"Just let me talk to him. Please."

"Verfy welp."

"Thanks."

Sammaël opened its eyes and gritted its jaw. That had been decidedly unpleasant. It tried not to think about the taste of its own blood, and tried not to think too much at all, because the headache was still there, along with the lingering feeling of dying, which was almost as bad.

"Sierra", it said.

"Oh, he's awake", the nurse said. "Can I ask—"

"I am... I'm alright", Sammaël said as it propped itself up. "My name is Abraham Douglas. Insurance is in order. Can I speak to Sierra in private, please?"

"You should be good to be discharged. How's your head?" the nurse asked, ignoring its question. Sammaël looked her in the eyes.

"A headache. I would appreciate something for the pain." Repeating the same words felt weird. Trite. Like it was wasting its time. On the other hand, trying to rush things hadn't gone that well.

The nurse nodded. "That should be covered. I'll be back in just a moment." She stood up and walked to the door. Sammaël looked at Sierra, who had been quiet this whole time.

"Sierra, can we talk?" it asked. She nodded.

"What happened, Abe?" her jaw was tight, and she looked at it with apprehension.

"A fight with your brother. I hit my head. He is fine." It sat on the edge of the bed then stood up on unsteady legs, feeling lightheaded for a moment, then ran a hand over its throat. The sensation of the knife going in was still fresh in its memory. Sierra just looked at it.

"Come on", she said. "You look like shit. I'll let you get cleaned up at my place. After that, I never want to see you again."

"There is more", Sammaël said. "Though perhaps that is best discussed in the car." The nurse came back in with a small cup and a glass of water. Sammaël took the painkiller with a thank you, and then they made for the exit. Sierra seemed lost in thought, staring straight ahead, right up until they got to her car.

"Morris already told me what happened", she said. "But thank you for being honest." She crossed her arms and glared at it. "Can't say you didn't have it coming, Abe."

"I am lucky Morris didn't kill me", Sammaël said. "For what I did."

"I — Yes. Exactly. What were you even *think-*

ing? Drinking? In Morris' watering hole? What did you think was going to happen?"

"Confrontation was inevitable", Sammaël said. "I was too far gone."

"Jesus fucking Christ. You must've hit your head pretty hard to be introspective like that", Sierra said, then her expression softened as she unlocked the car. That hint of concern was back again. "Take it easy. Look... I don't know what's going on with you Abe, and frankly, I don't know if I should care. But if this is some kind of cry for help."

"It is", Sammaël said. "I am not myself. I think the person I once was is dead."

"Yeah, well", Sierra said as she started the car, "I've heard that before." She looked over and frowned when Sammaël did its seatbelt. "Christ, you really aren't alright, are you? You're getting yourself killed at this rate."

"That's certainly within the realm of possibility", Sammaël said grimly. "Though I have every intention to keep that from happening. Sierra."

"Abe."

"I want to make things right. Do things right this time. I know that Ab— That I have hurt you in the past, and have said something to this effect before. You have been hurt. It is not my intention to shy away from the harm you and your family have suffered, but to avoid further harm, and maybe heal some of what was done."

"Just like that? You can't be fucking serious, Abe. And don't use the passive voice with me. Own up to what *you* did. To me. On my fucking *Wedding Day,* Abe."

"I am serious", Sammaël said. "Then perhaps, the first thing you deserve is an apology." Sammaël tried to find the right words. Should it keep up the pretense of being Abraham Douglas? That felt disingenuous. "You did not deserve any of it", it said. "Your wedding, your reputation, was ruined, and I'm sorry. Genuinely, truly." It took a deep breath. "I know this can not be simply fixed with words, and needs actions, but I hope that I can help you find healing and closure."

"What the *fuck",* Sierra mumbled. "Is this really *happening?* If this is some kind of play to

get back together, Abe, I'm going to fucking *kill—*"
Sammaël held up a hand.

"That... won't be necessary", it said, rubbing its neck again. "I have no intention of courting you. I only want to help. Not make things right, but to help you move forward, and maybe move forward with my own new... life."

"Why did y— hold on, why did you say it like that? Are you saying you had a near-death experience? If this is some kind of come-to-Jesus moment..."

"Something like that", Sammaël said. "I... I haven't been entirely honest with you." Her eyes immediately turned from calm yet confused to furious and her mouth became a thin line. "No, not... quite like that. You see... You could say I no longer... identify with the man Abraham Douglas."

"Y— You *what?*" They'd just arrived at the house, but Sierra still hit the brakes a little too hard, and then stared at it like it had grown a second head.

"I am not Abraham Douglas, the man you

once knew, who left you at the altar."

"Elaborate, and you had better not be messing with me."

"I am not messing with you", Sammaël said. "For a brief moment, after being hit by your brother, there was nothing. Blackness. Abraham Douglas died, and what... took his place was me. You could say there wasn't much ego there to begin with—" Sierra scoffed. Sammaël didn't quite understand where the humor was there, so it pushed on. "—but I had to construct something from scratch. And what was constructed is... *not* Abraham Douglas."

"So... who is it, then?" Sierra said, still eyeing it suspiciously.

"I am still learning that myself", Sammaël said, looking at its hands. "But there is a lot of history associated with this body, this person, and I think I can not move forward without fixing that first. I thought I had an idea of how to do that, but then..." It thought back to Sierra slipping in the bathroom. "I think I do not, and that's what I may need help with." It saw itself in the mirror in the sun visor overhead. "This facial hair must go, though. Whoever this is", it said, pointing at itself, "does not want facial hair."

"I thought... you would never shave off that rat on your upper lip. I've got a trimmer in my bathroom upstairs, if you're serious about this. Is this... real?" They both got out of the car. Sammaël was pretty happy with the way the conversation was going, and Sierra seemed to be much more receptive to him this time.

"Absolutely", Sammaël said. "Abraham Douglas is dead."

"Then what's... your name?"

"Sammaël", Sammaël said.

"I... Wh— Okay, you know what, sure. I mean... It explains why you were such a shithead before." She gave it a side-eye that made it very clear that she was keeping the possibility that it was still a shithead in the front of her mind and that it would be called out at the first sign of shitheadery.

"Wait, it does?" Sammaël frowned. That didn't make sense. It hadn't *actually* been Abraham.

Sierra shrugged as she opened the front door. "Yeah, I mean, if you're transgender…"

"What's transgender?"

"What?"

"What?"

Chapter 5

HEAR THE JAZZ GO DOWN

Sierra sipped her tea, looking intently at Sammaël over the rim of the mug. It held its own mug in its hands, glancing up at her occasionally, unsure about what to do, an experience it was getting uncomfortably familiar with*.

"Genuinely, Sammaël, I'm impressed", she finally said when she put the mug down. "I hadn't expected you to come to your conclusion about being trans without having encountered it before. Almost as impressed with *you* of all people not knowing about and having an opinion about trans people."

Sammaël looked through Abraham's memories, but there was no real mention of the word saved in there, other than the occasional muttering from an unobserved television. "It seems the feeling was too... present to ignore", it finally

---

*Having a human brain helps with choice paralysis the same way having your feet encased in cement helps with deep sea diving.

said. "Even if I didn't have the words to describe it." Sierra walked forward and put a hand on its shoulder.

"Well, I can't say you're, like, forgiven for all the shit you pulled", she continued, "but I feel like I can trust you when it comes to this. I can't put my finger on it, but I'm just... inclined to believe you, Sam— Actually, can I call you Sam? Sammaël is a bit of a mouthful, and it has a kind of... biblical feel to it."

"Thank you", Sammaël said, "and... yes, of course. Sam." It rolled the name over in its mouth like a dissolving pill. "Sam. I like that, I think."

"Nice. Alright, Sam, do you know what to do next?" Sierra asked as she walked around the room, tapping something into her phone. "Because I only have a tangential idea."

"I can not say I do", Sammaël said. "Although I presume altering the state of my body is something that should be within my capabilities." It thought back to the changes it had made to its eyes. It should be possible to do something like that to the rest of the body, shouldn't it? It just had to figure out how.

"Not on your own, you're not", Sierra said to Sammaël's surprise. "I'm not letting you self-medicate without supervision. You've gone down that road before and we know what lies at the end of it." She gave it a sideways glance, then held up her phone. "Anyway, this thread on Reddit says that experimenting with pronouns and gender expression is a good way to get started. What do you think?"

Tempted as it was to respond "More than you could possibly imagine", Sammaël felt like that wasn't going meaningfully advance the conversation. "Pronouns sound interesting", it said. "Can you elaborate?"

"Well, right now, I used male pronouns for you, right?" Sierra said. "When people talk about you, they say, like 'Oh, Douglas, *he's* an insufferable prick', or 'Oh, yeah, that's not *his* bottle of wine, *he* just took that from our liquor cabinet.' You know, stuff like—"

"I see", Sammaël interrupted, and it became acutely aware of a new physical sensation. Its chest felt tight, and there was a strange heat permeating throughout its upper body, spreading to its cheeks. "That isn't how I think about myself", it said. "Definitely not with those pronouns."

It thought for a minute. Gendered pronouns were a novel concept. On the one hand, it had been happy to think of itself as a being beyond personhood, beyond space, time, conception and as a result, beyond gender. But it was being drawn inexplicably towards one of them, at least.

"Well", Sierra said, "how *do* you think about yourself? What pronouns would you like me and others to use when we're talking about you?" She looked back down at her phone. "Jesus, there's loads. I don't even know how to pronounce some of these. But yeah, what are you thinking? Girl? Girl-adjacent? Neither boy nor girl?"

"I am... unsure", Sammaël said, mulling the idea over in its head. "Can we come back to that later? I need to think. What about the other thing? Gender expression?"

"Oh, yeah, of course", Sierra said. "Sorry, I didn't mean to pressure you. Anyway, uh, gender expression is changing your appearance in some way or another to be more in line with the gender you feel you might be. I think. Hold on." She scrolled a bit more, frowning.

"Such as shaving?" Sammaël offered. Sierra looked up and pointed.

"Exactly. Like shaving. You can do that, if you like. There's shaving supplies in the bathroom if you like." Sammaël looked over at the bathroom door and frowned. On the one hand, it wanted quite strongly to be rid of the facial hair, but on the other hand, that hadn't gone very well last time.

"I... Yes", it said, "although perhaps you should take a shower *first*." Sierra looked at it with a mixture of shock, confusion, and annoyance.

"Wow, okay, you spent the night in the hospital after passing out in an alley, I'm not sure you should be the one to tell me to take a shower, buddy", she said.

"No, no", Sammaël said quickly, realizing how what it had said would come off without context. It was going to have to do something it was rapidly gaining experience with: lie. "It is only that I've seen you look at the bathroom door a few times, and with all the stress associated with Ab— with me, I understand that a hot shower could be a good way to wash some of that off."

"Oh... Well, you're not wrong", Sierra said, "I had been thinking about it. Alright, fine, I'll see you in just a little bit." She took a few steps to the bathroom. "This isn't a ploy to get me out of the room, is it, Sam?" She leaned on the back of the sofa. "I really want to believe you, here, but if this turns out to be one of your..."

"It isn't", Sammaël said, enjoying the way she said its name, even when she wasn't trusting it. "Could I turn the radio on?" Sierra smiled slightly.

"Yeah", she said, "you can. I'll see you in just a bit." After a minute, the sound of running water came from behind the closed bathroom door, and Sammaël sat down on the sofa again, looking at its reflection in the dormant television.

Gender expression. What a concept. What would this body look like with feminine gender expression? Without Sammaël's help, would it even be worth trying? It knew what Abraham Douglas' face looked like without facial hair, but it still looked... wrong, somehow. It imagined the body in the reflection wearing Sierra's clothing, and immediately it recoiled, without knowing why. It felt almost... profane to think about that way. But the thought of seeing someone like Sierra in the reflection on the other hand, made it feel that heat on its face again. This time without the tightness in the chest.

"Sam", it said to itself, mulling it over. "Abraham. He. Sammaël. It. Sam. She." It frowned. Why was this hard? Why did it even care? It was supposed to be an all-powerful dimensionless entity beyond human comprehension, it shouldn't be having trouble with *grammar*. Also, it needed to find a way to explain to Sierra what it was, because pretending it was just Abraham Douglas with some self-reflection wasn't sustainable. It considered doing the eye-thing again, but thought better of it[†].

[†] A pocket-knife to the throat has that effect on people.

Perhaps there was another way. Its ability to change the color of its eyes proved that it was able to affect reality on a local level, and there was also its ability to alter the flow of time, even if its grasp thereof was a little tenuous at the moment. There *had* to be something, right?

As it pondered, it started to pace around the room, and realized it had barely been listening to the music, and that was frustrating it, too. It was here *to* listen to music. Music was the whole *point* of this experiment, and now its confusion about its identity and desire to make Sierra less uncomfortable with it was taking up so much mental real estate it wasn't even able to get *that* done.

"Hrmf", it said and shoved its hands in its pockets. That seemed to make it feel a little better, even if it couldn't put its finger on why that was. Looking out the window, it ignored the faint outline of its own reflection in the glass. This whole human thing was proving to be a lot more complicated than it was anticipating.

"You okay?" Sierra asked, drying her hair.

Sammaël nodded as it turned around. "You can use the bathroom if you want", she continued, already dressed.

One unpleasant shaving experience later, and Sammaël stepped out of the bathroom, running its hand across its throat, and jawline, continuously finding imperfections, a signature rasping feeling that made it want to peel off its face entirely and start over from scratch. If it had been in its full form and ability, that would have been a piece of cake.

But that was neither here nor there at the moment. Doing its best not to focus on that particular feeling anymore, it approached Sierra, who was swiping away on her phone in the recliner. "Sierra", it said. She opened her mouth in response, but it took her a second to respond. Sammaël assumed it was because she was still getting used to the new name. The pause was short, and would have meant nothing in any other context, but it could tell what was happening.

"Sam", she said, "what's up? What's next? Have you had some time to think?"

"I have", Sammaël said. "But first I think there is something we... that *I* need to get out of the way." It sat down on the sofa across from her, and looked around to see if her purse was nearby. Just in case. "I am aware I'll be asking a lot of you, but please, bear with me and keep an open mind. You have already shown a great capacity to do so, but I am asking for just a bit more."

Sierra put her phone down and leaned forward, elbows on her knees, and nodded. "Okay. I'm not sure where you're going with this, but let's hear it."

Sammaël felt *anxious.* It was apprehensive about having to go through this *again*, sure, and ideally it would like to avoid being stabbed again, but it also wanted to do right by Sierra. It wanted to be honest with her, and maybe help her move on from what was done by Abraham. Not to think that it was the same person as the man she had once loved.

But to get that right, it had to tread carefully. Sierra *was* an open-minded person, but of all the people in the world, the one she was most mistrustful and skeptical towards now sat across from her. Or at least, someone who looked exactly like him.

"We... There was a conversation, a year ago", Sammaël said, picking its words carefully, "about extraterrestrial life and concepts like god." Sierra took a moment but clearly remembered it, nodding. "Do you remember what you said?"

She mulled it over in her head for a second, and then responded with a smile. "*There are more things in heaven and earth, Horatio, than are dreamed of in your philosophy.* I remember you being pretty skeptical. Why?"

"Well..." Sammaël said, "what if there was proof? How would you respond to the existence of something... higher?" It frowned. Sure, its intellect was vast, larger than the combined intelligence of every other creature in the universe, but it didn't like thinking of itself as *higher.* "Or other, rather."

"Well... I'd have a *lot* of questions, that's for sure. Where are you going with this, Sam? Are you saying you've had some kind of... supernatural experience?" She frowned again. The skepticism was seeping in.

"Something like that", Sammaël said. "What if I did? What if I had proof? What if I asked you to trust me, so that I can show you?"

"Well, I'd ask you what you did to the real Abraham", she said with a laugh, and then caught herself. "Or Sam, sorry."

"That's alright", Sammaël said, but there seemed to be something stuck in the back of its throat. "You see... I didn't do anything to Abraham. But I was... understating when I said I wasn't Abraham anymore." It looked her in the eyes. "If I could present proof to you, right now, what would you say? What would you do?"

"I'd... have to take a moment to process that. What kind of proof? Much as I want to believe you, I'd like to get an idea beforehand, if it's all the same to you."

"Understanding", Sammaël said. "I am not, and have *never* been Abraham Douglas. When I say these next few words, I need you to believe me, and I *will* show you." It reached out a hand

and held it open, then nodded at Sierra, who very hesitantly put hers in it. "I chose the name Sammaël, not because I didn't want to be Abraham, but because a name was something that I have never had a need for before. I am not the person you think I am. Until recently, I may not have been a person at all."

If Sammaël had been anything, it had been a consciousness, maybe even *the* consciousness, given form. Power. Hunger. It had been a singular entity of Identity. Consciousness and perception were the foundational blocks of its entire existence. Creating an identity to live in a human body had been as easy as creating any other kind of life.

So passing just a little bit of it on to Sierra, even in this greatly diminished form, was not nearly beyond its ability. It shared, across the physical connection of their hands, a fraction of a fraction of its identity, and braced. There was the possibility that she'd take it badly, that she'd scream or go mad, or that her brain would dribble unceremoniously out of her ears. It hoped it hadn't overdone i—

"Oh!" Sierra said, "I felt something! How did you do that?"

Okay. It was going to have to turn it up just a little bit. Turning up the proverbial dial, Sammaël opened its identity to Sierra.

Chapter 6

YOU WERE PART OF A DREAM

"Sam."

"Sierra."

"What is happening?"

"Your consciousness is expanding. Allow it to. Take your time."

"Why do I taste whipped cream and straw-berries?"

"That's the seventh dimension."*

"Is that why I smell toast?"

"No, you are smelling toast because you're having several strokes per second."

"Um", Sierra said, and frowned. Sammaël gently patted the back of her hand. Human minds were almost as frail as their bodies, but thankfully, here and now, it had at least a little bit of control

---

*This is true for every species capable of transcending to the seventh, and nobody knows why.

over what was happening, and it could keep Sierra from keeling over, at least.

"Do not worry. I'll guide you through to the other side. Just do not let go."

"Uh. Gotcha." Sammaël felt Sierra squeeze its hand a little tighter. She was clearly worried, but it wasn't planning on letting her drown in the spaces between the cosmos and the one next to it. Especially not considering it was the one that had brought her here. "Sam?" she asked. It squeezed her hand back, enjoying the gentle warmth of their fingers against each other.

"Yes?"

"I'm scared to open my eyes", Sierra said. Sam looked at her. Her closed eyes were visibly flickering back and forth, trying to look at all the information an expanded mind was projecting on the back of her eyelids. "I'm worried the world will terrify me. Or I'll go crazy."

"It will not", Sammaël said. "You will not. This may not be *very* comforting, but it may help you to know that you are now a step closer to being the kind of thing the world is, traditionally, scared of."

"It's not, no!" Sierra said. "What does that mean? Did I grow tentacles?" Her eyes flew open and she looked down at herself, and then made eye contact with Sammaël. It felt a strange noise coming from its own mouth, and immediately clamped it shut, until it realized it had laughed involuntarily. "I'm fi—" Sierra said sheepishly, interrupting herself to look at the air around her. "Oh."

"Take your time", Sammaël said. "If this is overwhelming, I may be able to dial these experiences back to a more agreeable scale."

"No, it's fine", Sierra said as she held a hand up. "I think I can see time."

"Interesting." Sammaël observed her for a moment. "Ordinarily, one can only observe fourth-dimensional parallel motion when moving perpendicular to the stream."

"What do you *mean* ordinarily?" she said, and looked at Sam. A realization started to dawn on her. "You were never Abraham, were you?" Sammaël shook its head.

"No, I wasn't. I think you are ready. Close your eyes."

"What am I going to see?"

"How I see the universe", it said. "And how it sees me." Slowly, Sammaël allowed its vision, the fullness of its being and perception, to flow into her. For the first time in her life, through closed eyes, Sierra became aware of the universe. Tears started to roll down her cheeks.

"Sam", she said. "It's beautiful."

"It is."

"There's so *much* of it. All at once."

"There is."

They sat in silence. Sure, human beings had seen the stars, but very few people ever lie down on the grass, far away from the pollution of light, and look up at the night sky, and see the full infinity of the universe. Few people experience the vertigo of what it is like to be fully *untethered*. And even those who have, have never seen what the universe is *actually* like. It's like trying to see the shape of a balloon from the inside.[†]

"Is this how you see the world?"

"It used to be. Now I'm here." There. The last step. With a deep breath, which Sierra mirrored, Sammaël turned the vision inward. Before, it had shown her what the universe looked like to a being for whom dimensions were more like suggestions and planets were snacks. Now, it was time to show her what that being looked like. With more than a little trepidation, Sammaël revealed to her the magnitude of its being.

"Oh."

"Yes."

"That's you?"

"The part that isn't in here."

"Oh."

"What are you?"

"There is no word for what I am. I simply am."

"How old are you?"

"Older than time itself."

[†] And almost as suffocating.

"That doesn't... how..."

"I simply am, Sierra."

"Why didn't you show me this before?"

"I tried to. You stabbed me in the throat."

"No, I didn't."

"Not this time, no", Sam said, trying not to sound bitter. Sierra sat in silence for a while, until Sammaël was starting to get worried that maybe her brain had turned into soup after all. "Sierra?"

"Yes, sorry. This is a lot." Sierra opened her eyes. There were stars in them. "This is real, isn't it?" she said, and looked at Sammaël in a way nobody ever had. Nobody had ever *seen* it, not really.[‡] And nobody had ever looked at it with something other than fear or revulsion. But Sierra seemed interested. Fascinated.

"It is", Sammaël said, taking note of the fact that she still hadn't let go of its hand. "How are you feeling?" It had never had a conversation before this day. Sure, it had, once upon a time, spoken to mortal creatures on various planets.

[‡] Not without going spectacularly insane, at least.

Usually, a cult popped up a few days later, and usually they would try to start summoning it. It was exhausting.

Not only had it had a conversation, but for the first time in its eons-long life Sammaël had opened itself up to another being. It had trusted someone with itself, and with how it saw the world.

"I'm... confused. Scared. I don't know what's going on. I don't know who you are. Does that mean Abraham really *is* dead?" she asked. Sammaël nodded. "I can tell. You're not him. He's not in there, in your eyes. I can see it." She squeezed its hand again. It was a welcome touch.

"That's r—" Sammaël started, but a low rumbling interrupted it. It looked around. "The room is shaking", it said just as the cups started to rattle. "Strange. That's not supposed t—"

"I don't think that was you", Sierra said, standing up and walking over to the window on slightly unsteady legs. Sam followed her as more and more items in the room began to rattle and move. "That's weird, we don't get earthquakes h—" She fell backwards, Sammaël catching her in its arms. The floor underneath them rose, as if it was a blanket on the back of a whale. Splinters filled the air as it shattered. Sammaël had the presence of mind to toss itself to one side and Sierra to the other, ignoring the signals of pain the frail body was barraging its brain with. "Sam!" Sierra yelled.

Sammaël looked over just in time to see a part of the building start to peel away. The part Sierra was on. As if in slow-motion, she was starting to fall away. Sam threw itself forward, knocking the wind out of its body as it landed roughly, and in that moment, it didn't care. It felt pure unadulterated relief for the first time in its life when its hand closed on her wrist, and then pure unadulterated pain when its shoulder was yanked almost out of its socket. "Do not—" it groaned, barely able to breathe, "don't let go!"

Sierra wasn't wasting her breath, and latched onto its arm, pulling herself up as half of her apartment crashed into the street behind her. That's when Sammaël saw it. It wasn't an earthquake. There was a massive sinkhole where the street used to be, a gaping maw swallowing chunks of the surrounding buildings.

Sammaël felt its shoulder pop as Sierra pulled herself up and onto the ledge. They scrambled away from the gap, neither of them caring about the scrapes and splinters they'd both suffered. The floor lurched as the building fell apart behind them, plaster and wood crumbling away. "What", Sierra gasped as they leaned against the far wall, "is happening?". The floor felt somewhat stable here, and Sammaël's arm hung limply by its side.

"I do not know", it said, and shoved the arm back into its socket, knocking the wind out of its body *again*. And breathing was already unpleasant. "Ow", it hissed through its teeth. "I did not enjoy that. These bodies are spectacularly imperfect."

"Jesus, Sam, did you just... What is *happening?*"

"This isn't right", Sammaël said with a groan. "Everything is *wrong*. We should get downstairs. I don't trust the rest of this building not to come down on us." Sierra nodded and pulled it up by its good arm.

Leading the way down the stairs, Sierra helped keep Sammaël steady as they avoided more and more falling debris. There were people screaming in the distance, muffled by the sound of shattering stone, falling glass and distant sirens. Every breath hurt. They saw just as they were about to make their way to the bottom floor. The front door was gone, same as the street and a chunk of the building. Sammaël sat down, massaging its shoulder. Even if they had to get out as quickly as possible, it needed a breather. "I don't suppose you have a back door?"

"No dice", Sierra said, looking around. "Maybe we can get to a neighboring building from the roof?" She looked up just in time for a giant piece of plaster to fall down and explode between them.

"That roof?" Sammaël said dryly as it stood back up. "Maybe we can—" it said, when the wall fell over, outward, into the building next door. Whatever it had been, it was rapidly becoming flat. "That works", it said, and Sierra quickly hurried over to help it climb over the rubble. The further they were from the sinkhole, the more comfortable it was getting.

Whatever had just caused the sinkhole to appear and everything to go wrong, right now the most important part was putting some distance between them and it. "Careful", Sierra said as she helped it through what had at some point been a glass storefront. They stepped onto the street. It was chaos. The sinkhole was larger than Sammaël at first thought it was, and seemed to still be expanding some.

"How did this happen?" Sierra said as she looked up at her building. "Ughh. My *stuff!*"

"You don't seem... particularly upset", Sammaël said. "I'd think... I feel like losing all your belongings would be more... more." Sierra looked at it and shrugged.

"It's just stuff. I can get more stuff", she said. "The important thing is that we both made it out alive, that we're both safe. Besides, whatever Abe didn't break, he pawned. I'm used to not putting a lot of value in things." Despite her knowing Sammaël wasn't *him*, it still felt the urge to apologize. "Still, though. I'll miss my bed." She patted her pocket. "I've got my phone and my credit cards, so we'll have a place to stay."

"You're remarkably calm", Sammaël said. "Not that I mind."

"I've recently had someone expand my understanding of the universe", Sierra said with a smile as she turned back to it. "Let's just say that it's given me some perspective."

"Ah", Sammaël said. "I am... I'm glad I could help."

"I am too, Sam", Sierra said. "Now, let's get out of here." She looked at the hole, and started walking away from it. "Just in case that thing expands. I think I need somewhere to sit down, and I want to have a look at your shoulder. Maybe a hotel."

"That would be good", Sammaël said. Just then, the floor trembled again, an aftershock, and Sammaël fell to its knees. There was a whistling noise. Sam stood back up just in time to see Sierra look down at her chest. There was a red spot on her shirt, and it was slowly expanding. In the middle of the red spot was a little gray point. She touched it with her finger.

"Huh", she said as she fell forward into Sammaël's arms, an arrow sticking out of her back. Behind her, from a second story window, a shocked-looking teenager with headphones lowered his bow.

"You have *got* to be kidding me!" Sam screamed as Sierra died in its arms.

Chapter 7

BEFORE SHE NEVER
SEEMED TO CARE

Sammaël looked over at the teenager, and briefly considered walking over there and turning their brain into soup. It would be easy. All Sammaël would have to do was reveal itself, across every single dimension it existed on, even the ones that smelled like old socks,* and their head would pop like a grape.

Then it looked down at Sierra, and the strange *feelings* looking at her body brought to the surface, and then back up. The child seemed to sense *something* was off. Maybe Sammaël had begun to emanate a sense of foreboding — it did that, sometimes. It could smear the offender's mind across seventeen realities, and then someone would find it and feel the same way the way Sammaël felt when it looked at Sierra. It wasn't worth it.

---

*Especially the ones that smelled like old socks.

That, and it wasn't going to matter. With more care than was necessary, Sammaël put the body down. It didn't know why it did that. Sierra was gone, after all, so why was it showing reverence to her body? Whatever the reason, Sam gently set her down on the sidewalk, then stood up and grabbed temporal linearity by the throat.

"I'm telling you I *am* a relative."

"What family?"

"I'm their fiancee."

"He didn't mention a fia—"

"It's complicated. Just let us talk. Please."

"Very well."

"Thank you."

Sammaël blinked its eyes open. A part of it wanted to resent the fluorescent lights on the ceiling, but at this point they were a welcome sight. And Sierra's voice was like a balm anyway. It sat upright. "Abe Douglas", it said to the nurse, who seemed satisfied. Something about calling itself Abraham left a sour taste in its mouth, competing for parking space with the various other unpleasant tastes. "Engaged to Sierra Guthrie.

I'm fine. My insurance information is in order. I would like a painkiller, if it's all the same to you." It ignored the pounding in its head for a moment to look at Sierra, standing and breathing and *alive*. "It's good to see you, Sierra", Sam said.

"You too", Sierra said with a very forced smile as the nurse stood up and walked out. "I'm going to want an explanation." Sammaël frowned and stood up with a slight nod.

"Of course", it said with a resigned sigh. "I am happy to explain everything that happened. There was a fight w—"

"I know all that, Sam", Sierra interrupted, and Sammaël froze to the spot, then slowly turned to her. Sierra looked like she'd seen a ghost, ironically. "Yeah", she said with a nod.

Sammaël shook its head, which was something of a mistake. "You remember?"

"I do." Her voice was a loud whisper. "What the *fuck* Sam? I died!"

"Why do you remember?" Sammaël answered. "That's not how this is supposed to work!" It looked her up and down. "Everything?"

"Yes!" Sierra said and held her hand up. "I can *still* see time flowing between my fingers if I squint! I *died!!* Am I just supposed to breeze past that?"

"Uh", Sammaël said, "for now, probably." The nurse came in with a small cup with a painkiller in it. Snatching the cup out of her hand with a quick thank you on the way out, Sammaël wracked its brain. "I don't understand. This doesn't make any sense."

Sierra rushed to keep pace with it. "Can you tell me what the hell is going on here?" She grabbed it by the arm. On the one hand, Sammaël wanted to oblige her and explain everything, but it also wanted to get out of the hospital and get somewhere safe. It wasn't looking forward to finding out what other ridiculous combination of circumstances could kill them next time. But not telling her wouldn't be fair. She'd died twice already.

"Okay", Sammaël said. "You remember everything? You remember who I am? What I am?" It rubbed a hand over its jaw, immediately regretted it as the tough bristles of its facial hair pricked its fingers, and made a sound of disgust.

Sierra nodded. "Yes", she said, "I do. Massive, unknowable entity from beyond the edges of time and space with a love of earth music, a curious streak, and bad dysphoria."

"Okay... yes. Probably", Sammaël said, shaking its head as it started to move down the hall again (to Sierra's annoyance). "I don't want to stay here", it explained. "The lights hurt my eyes." The doors to the hospital's exit opened to fresh air and much less unpleasant lighting. It stopped. "Look", it said. "When I first revealed myself to you, you died."

"I know!" Sierra said. "I got impaled! I was there!"

"No", Sam said, "No, that wasn't the first time."

"*What?*"

"The first time, you slipped in the bathroom and cracked your skull", it said. Sierra's mouth fell open. "The second time, you killed me with the pocket knife in your purse.

"Wh—" Sierra said. "I... Wh— *Why?* You know what, it doesn't matter. Why don't I remember those?"

"I don't know", Sammaël said as it walked to her car. "Anyway, after the first time, I decided that I had to do something, so I reversed my place in temporal space, and decided to start over. Maybe, because I showed you the flow of time, your consciousness is a little... untethered now. Which is why you remember."

"How do you know that? Do you do this often? How many p—"

"I've never done this before", Sammaël said. "I never even had a proper conversation with a sentient being before I *met* you, Sierra. I'm going off my understanding of the various laws of the universe and my gut feeling."

"You are a very weird eldritch abomination", Sierra said with a scoff and opened the door for them both.

"So my mom keeps telling me", it said with a sigh as it threw itself down in the passenger seat, and then caught Sierra's shocked look. "That was a joke. I don't have a mother that I know of. I was birthed from the very concepts before time released itself from the infinitely small point that was the universe."

"Sure", Sierra said. "So now what? We can't go to my apartment, because it's about to fall into a sinkhole." She shook her head. "Do you think we have time to go in there and grab some of my old records? I have a signed vinyl of Blonde on Blonde..."

"I don't think so", Sammaël said. "I would rather not risk either of us dying again. "Why are you so calm about this? You died, and you *remember* it, and now I tell you that I've gone through this loop three times and you shrug it off." The car started with a slight jolt, jostling Sammaël's slightly abused brain.

"Sam", Sierra said. "As a species, we've been writing time loop stories since forever. I grew up watching *Groundhog Day*. I rewatched *Russian Doll*, like, a couple of months ago. It's not that complex of a concept to wrap your head around when you can *see time!*"

"Is that still happening?" Sammaël asked with a frown as they left the parking lot. "I can do something about that, if you like. I don't want you to have to ignore it all the time."

Sierra shook her head. "No", she said. "It's only there if I focus. Besides, it's not unpleasant to look at. The color's pretty. Like a kind of purple-orange-greenish." She seemed to chew her thoughts for a moment. "What do we do now? Where are we going?"

"I don't know", Sammaël said, "but something is wrong. I'm starting to worry that someone — or some*thing* — knows I am here and is trying to stop me from existing here."

"You think someone's trying to kill you?" Sierra said as she turned down a street. "Alright, let's go to a hotel first. I need to sit down and think. Fuck, I need to call my parents."

"Maybe it's best if you go home to them for a few days", Sammaël said. "I will get to the bottom of this and stop whoever keeps making attempts on my life." It looked out the window with grim resolution as the streets rolled past. "I

97

don't understand. I haven't been to this corner of the galaxy in millennia, and I don't think I've *ever* set foot on it in this temporal stream. Who is after me?"

"Are you sure you're the only one like you?" Sierra asked.

"Yes. If there was another like myself, we would've struggled long before. I'm... very present. Well, my true form is." It looked down. "This one needs a little work, though. Speaking of which..." It looked at a convenience store. "Do you mind if we pick up some shaving supplies on our way to the hotel?"

Twenty minutes later, and it felt better with an electric shaver and a razor in its lap. The weight of them was strangely comforting. It wasn't going to help them stop whatever was trying to assassinate Sammaël, but something about the purchases were like a weight off its shoulders. Half an hour later, it was looking at itself in the mirror of a motel bathroom, wiping off the last of the shaving cream.

"Yeah", Sierra said from the bed, "love you

too." She hung up the phone and then blew raspberries. "Do you have any idea where to get started?" Sammaël thought as it tossed the cheap towel aside.

"Nothing I can think of, off the top of my head", it said. "This would be a lot easier if I was in my full form, of course", it said. "I could read the thoughts of the entire planet, follow the streams of consciousness of civilization."

"So I have a question", Sierra said, putting her hands behind her head. "You talk about your true form. Where is it right now? What's it doing? Are you two separate? Is it just sort of... hanging out?"

"It's not a separate entity", Sammaël said. "Think of it... Imagine you're looking at a live recording of a distant location. You can argue that your consciousness is in that location, in a sense, right? You're seeing things from that location." Sierra jutted her jaw forward and nodded. "Imagine that, but with every aspect of your identity. I'm piloting this body", it waved down at itself, "and all sensory input is coming from it, but my essence is still out there, dormant."

"Then *why* can't you just take a step back from the camera?" Sierra asked. "If you're so powerful?" Sammaël sat down on the other bed and lowered its head onto the pillow. It wasn't a very good pillow, and the sheets were far too stiff[†]. But it was still a welcome reprieve.

"I'm worried I'd rip a hole in time and space", Sammaël said. "I'll have to drop the metaphor in favor of another one, but I already took a risk inhabiting Abraham. There is a *lot* of me, and human brains are very fragile. I worry that if I hop in and out, I might burst his mind *across every dimension*. Which would mean he likely wouldn't have survived childbirth." Sierra made a face. "Exactly."

"So you're stuck like this until... what? You're done?"

"Something like that", Sammaël said. "I could, in theory, just drop Abraham, figure out what is happening, and then find a different host, but..."

[†]The mysteries of motel laundry are considered forbidden knowledge, best lost to time.

It shrugged. "I want to make the best of this one. Besides." It looked over at Sierra and felt the corners of its mouth twitch. "I've only ever really met one human being, and I'd like to make the best of that, too."

Sierra smiled back. "You're a strange one, Sam. But... Thank you. So, there's nothing you can do?"

"Not *nothing*", Sammaël replied. "I can manipulate time, although there appears to be a hard limit. I can only go back as far as my waking up in the hospital, and only *to* that time." It looked at the ceiling. "I would like to try changing my form somewhat, but I'd rather it not go wrong. These things are very delicate."

"Hey", Sierra said. Sam looked over. "You'll figure it out", she said. "You seem pretty incredible, I doubt there's something you *couldn't* do."

"Thank you", Sammaël said, and smiled. Something in its lower chest bubbled happily.

Chapter 8

MYSELF AS PEOPLE SEE ME

"I have an idea", Sammaël said, to Sierra's fascinated horror. That wasn't because Sierra was against the idea of ideas, but because Sammaël had said it with the same excitement and inflection as mad scientists might talk about their new death laser. Still, she wanted to give it the benefit of the doubt, so she raised her eyebrows in an unspoken question. "So, if there really is someone hunting me", Sammaël continued, "they are doing so by focusing on this body." It waved generally at itself.

Now that they'd had a minute and the raw sensation of freshly-shaven face was ebbing away, it had been easier to pretend like the body hadn't really been there, to distance itself from it a little bit. Sadly, thinking about it too much made every uncomfortable sensation edge its way back into its mind like a cat pushing itself through a barely open door. It pushed the strange feelings to the back of its mind,* and continued.

"Additionally, I believe whatever is doing this, can only recognize me by the tether to my host body. So, I will simply... try to inhabit the body itself more", it continued. "Reduce the link between my real body and this one as much as I can. Step inside the proverbial television screen, as it were."

"Are you sure that's a good idea?" Sierra asked. "What if you can't go back?"

"I will not let that happen", Sammaël replied. "The tether *can not* be broken by anything or anyone but myself. But I can make it so imperceptible it might as well not be there."

Sierra paced around the small motel room, her hands in her pockets. It was clear to Sammaël she was worried about something. "Will there be any... side effects?"

"None I can immediately foresee. My experience", it said, "should be no different than it has been. If anything, we should be considerably safer

---

*Don't do this at home. Have you tried yoga?

for the immediate future." Sierra nodded, but clearly wasn't convinced yet. "It will not require much. Only a brief moment of concentration. You can stay here with me if you like." It sat cross-legged on the bed, back against the wall.

"I... Do you want me to stay?" Sierra asked. Sammaël looked at her for a moment.

"I would like that, yes."

"Then say that", she said with a grin, and sat on the foot of the bed, also crossing her legs. "If I can help at all, even if it's just by being here, then I'd like you to speak your mind."

"That's very kind of you", Sammaël said, smiling faintly.

"Well, I mean", Sierra mused, "if I can do something to avoid getting shot again... I wouldn't be opposed to preventing my own death again, you know?" She laughed sheepishly, then reached out and put a hand on Sammaël's. "But I *am* here for you."

With a grateful smile, Sammaël nodded, then closed its eyes. It reached out to its body, still out there in space, the dark side of the moon, a shadow the size of a planet, skulking. It was strange, like watching itself in a mirror but... not. Its consciousness — not to mention its abilities — were extremely limited like this, but that was okay.

Existence, for a creature like Sammaël, was not something that needed to be theorized. It was not just a certainty of feeling, or a thought experiment. "I think, therefore I am", was the kind of thing mortal creatures needed to reconcile their insecurities about the universe. By contrast, Sammaël had *proof* of its own existence. Its own tangible reality was something that could be spun out like silk thread, molded into a human brain if needed.

And for now, it stretched that silk thread to its limits. Nothing but itself would ever see it, so infinitesimally thin it might as well be said to not exist at all, and yet with a tensile strength that could cut a star in half. It kept as much of its consciousness inside the body as it could. That was the main goal, after all, despite how much of it there really still was out there. It was like trying to pour a drop of water into a glass with a pipette the size of a skyscraper. But it managed. It was painstaking, filing away at the thread until the Sammaël was as much of a singular entity as possible, without severing the connection entirely.

"Sam?"

The sound of its name was strange to hear like this, like someone was talking to it from the other side of thick glass. It realized it had deliberately taken that distance from its own body again, and that it did have to slip back into the body of what had once been Abraham Douglas again.

"Sam?"

Sammaël realized it was putting things off. Sure, it wanted to go back to being around Sierra; she made it feel safe. But that also meant going back into that *body,* and the thought made its skin crawl, the thought of running its hand over its jaw and feeling the rough stubble, of looking down and seeing the rough hands. Of seeing that face in the mirror.

"Sam!!"

It opened its eyes. That was strange. It had expected to see Sierra at the foot of the bed, where it had left her, but she wasn't. It didn't know where Sierra was, because it was staring at the underside of the bed. Slowly, it became aware of the pain in its arms and relaxed. Immediately, its hands were pried away, something that was more difficult than it should be.

"Sammaël!" Sierra's voice came from somewhere to its left. It looked up at her. She was standing over it as she tried to keep it from digging its nails any further into its arms and shoulders. "What's wrong? What's happening?"

"I—" it said, and the sound of its own voice was like a sledgehammer to the brain. No longer something to be ignored, it physically hurt to hear even a single syllable pass through its own lips. This was *wrong*, on so many levels, and there was nothing it could do to alleviate it.

Well, that wasn't true. It slowly started to pull away from the body again, and realized there was nowhere *to* go. Not without disrupting the work it had done to hide itself. It faced the

choice between painting a target on its own —
and Sierra's — back, or... this. It was not an easy
choice to make. Feeling her hand on its back
helped, though, and it relaxed again.

"Try to breathe", Sierra said. "I think you're...
okay?"

"I am", Sammaël managed, trying to ignore
how rough the voice sounded. "Kind of." It sat
upright as she helped it back up onto the bed. "I
did it."

"Then what was all the—" Sierra made a
scratching motion at her arm, "—about?"

"I'm... more aware", it said. "A lot more. It's
harder to think... right." It rubbed its head. Even
words were coming out strangely. It was starting
to realize that, without its larger mind as 'close'
by, it had to rely more on Douglas' understanding
of language, which was imprecise at best. Even
that was a strangely disconcerting thought, the
idea that its mind was closer to that of Abraham.
Like being locked in a room with a cloud of toxic
spores, it tried not to breathe.

"I'm so sorry", Sierra said, and wrapped Sam-

108

maël in a very gentle hug, much to its surprise.

"For what?" it asked, although it also didn't really want to do anything that might end the hug.[†] Sierra seemed to pick up on it and squeezed a little tighter and didn't say anything, leaving Sammaël to enjoy the comfort and confusion.

It understood why things hurt more, to an extent. There had been a distance between mind and body before. If it had kept that distance deliberately, it couldn't say. But now that it wasn't there, it was keenly felt. Like taking a step and realizing too late it was off the edge of a cliff, Sammaël was suddenly in an emotional and sensory free-fall. And the worst part was that it felt like the ghost of Abraham Douglas, douchebag so prolific he should've gone professional, was right there with him.

He was in every reflection, hiding in Sammaël's words and even memories, which no longer felt like something to be absent-mindedly

---

[†] Space, vast and mysterious and unknowable, does not have a lot of hugs in it.

flicked through but something *it* had done. The last thing it wanted was to be Abraham. It was vaguely aware of Sierra squeezing it a little tighter as its breathing became labored, gasping, rasping breaths interrupted by choked sobs that seemed to come out of nowhere.

It wasn't Abraham Douglas. But now, here, so far removed from what Sammaël had always been, it was starting to lose track of what Sammaël was. Of *who* Sammaël was. Was it even still the same entity? It had to be, right? If it wasn't, what was it? But if it really was the cosmically powerful entity Sammaël, why did it *feel* scared and small?

There was a moment, a *very* loud and tempting moment, where it considered giving up on the whole corporeal thing, and turn back to being Sammaël, rend the world apart and forget about this small ball of misery and noise and swim the cosmos again.

But then... there would be no more music. Not just for itself, but... in total. There would be no more music and nobody would ever be there to listen to it again. And there was Sierra, of course. Who was still holding it. If it had still been up there, wrapped around the moon like a shadowy blanket, would that decision have been easier? Was this Sammaël... *different?*

What if this wasn't Sammaël at all? What if Sierra had figured that out already? Sure, it was still cosmically strange, but it certainly wasn't powerful. It wasn't even able to do something about the body it was in. So what, then?

"What am I?" it mumbled, and realized that its voice didn't grate as much when it whispered. Sierra pulled away and looked at it, her hands still on its shoulders.

"I don't know", she said. "But I think you don't either, so maybe together we can figure it out." She smiled warmly, and it made Sammaël's chest feel weird. It was a little light-headed, too. "Well, I think we can rule out 'Abraham Douglas'," she quipped. "I only ever saw him cry once and that was to get a better deal on a second-hand car." She wiped away Sammaël's tears.

"Definitely not him", Sammaël growled. "Never him."

"Okay. So are you a cosmic entity on a joyride, here to listen to banging tunes?" Sammaël shook its head. Maybe originally, but things had changed. It had changed.

"Not anymore", it said. "I think I'm... different, now, but I can't understand why. This body feels like a... a *prison*. Like who I am is below the skin, that I need to peel it away in order to feel free, to feel whole again. But who I am is also not just... what I was."

"Something new?" Sierra said, tapping her lip. "Someone new?"

It thought about that for a moment. If this really was all new, and it didn't think like it used to, and it didn't *experience* things like it used to, then— "I... think so."

"Still Sammaël?" Sierra asked, raising an eyebrow.

"I don't know. Yes. No. Sam?" It liked Sam.

"Sam. I like Sam. Sam is nice, even if they're a little bit awkward", she said, giving another one of her trademark comforting smiles. "Even with all of the weird communication issues, getting to know Sam has been fun.

"I think... I think Sam might want to try some of those pronouns right about now", Sam said.

"Oh? And which ones are those?" Sierra's smile split into a wide grin.

"Well..." Sam said, and she smiled right back.

Three thousand two hundred and fifty-four miles away, after a series of technical failures and human errors, an airplane took off from a runway that wasn't supposed to.[‡]

[‡] Usually, this is still preferable to airplanes trying to land when they're not supposed to.

Chapter 9

SUPPOSE I NEVER EVER MET YOU

"Now what?"

"I'm not sure", Sam said. "I need... to relax, I think." Her entire upper body had been tensed up for... well, as long as she could remember. But now, disconnected from the eldritch entity that was technically still her, she was much more aware of her entire body.

That was... technically an improvement, like reaching under the cupboard and hearing — and feeling — the loud *SNAP* of a closing mousetrap; not having to worry about sticking one's hand in a mousetrap is an improvement.* And it had made the tension in Sam's body all the more tangible.

"Like... literally?" Sierra said. "Okay, I have a dumb idea, but you never know." She stepped

---

* "Fear of the Unknown" includes mousetraps, dropped thumbtacks, and missed phone calls from your mother.

off the bed and stretched. "So, this motel has a pool. It should be hot enough to be nice, and late enough for there not to be anyone else around." She looked at Sam, who tried her best to inform Sierra through arcane eyebrow movements that she was, at best, skeptical.

"I'm not sure undressing is going to help my physical discomfort, Sierra", Sam said. "No offense, but I can barely stand to look down as it is, I don't want to do so when I'm not... covered up." She looked at her hands and grimaced.

"No, I — Ugh, I'm so sorry. No, I meant just... sitting by the pool. Listening to the water. I'm sure the mini bar has some beers in it. I promise, it'll help you loosen up."

Sam nodded. That made some sense, at least. "If you say so", she said. Sierra did have a lot more experience being a human than Sam did, after all. And there *was* a mini fridge in the room, so that was a welcome discovery, although the prices were... extravagant.

A few minutes later they sat by a pool that was remarkably clean for how out-of-the-way the motel was, a cold beer in hand, looking up at the late evening sky. Sam's shoes and socks were a little off to the side, next to Sierra's, and their feet gently sloshed in the cool water.

Nothing needed to be said for a bit. She didn't particularly enjoy the taste of beer, which was a discovery all on its own. When she'd first slipped into this body, everything had been new and overwhelming and amazing, but now she was developing *tastes*.

Beer, she was coming to realize, was not... fantastic. It tasted mostly like unpleasant water. She wondered for a moment why people drank it at all, and then she moved her head. Her brain sort of lazily sloshed into place with a half second delay, and she immediately understood. It wasn't for everyone, but she was starting to get it now.

She looked over at Sierra, who was lying on her back with her hands behind her head and looking at the first few stars that were starting to peek through the pink-white-and-blue of the evening sky. Sam smiled.

"This *is* nice", she said, leaning back onto her

elbows. "Why is this nice?"

"I don't know", Sierra said. "Because you're not doing anything. Because water feels nice. Because there's no expectations and nothing that needs to be done *right now* and most people kind of... forget how to do nothing?" She propped herself up as well. "You look like you're getting the hang of it though."

"I think I am", Sam said. "I hope so. I don't know how much time we have, you know?"

"Try not to think about it", Sierra said. "Either your plan worked, and we'll have to figure out what to do with... everything, and then that can wait a day or two. Or it didn't, and then we die and you wake up in the hospital again, and we try something else."

"I wouldn't even know what to try", Sam said. "Well, nothing short of abandoning 'Sam' altogether and swimming away from this little blue planet forever." She raised her bottle at Sierra. "And I'm not ready to do that yet."

She almost dropped the beer when she felt Sierra's hand on her back. "I'm glad. I'd like to get to know you better." She sat up. "Speaking of which... what *is* there to know about the great and terrible Sammaël?"

"I'm... not sure where to start, really", Sam said. "It all feels so cosmically... insignificant, and yet."

"And yet, it would blow my tiny mind?"

"Something like that", Sam chuckled. "I was... terrifying. When I was younger I traumatized more than one young civilization, although I never did go in for any of the world-devouring." She paused. "I was worshiped as a god, once. That was interesting, although their prayers were a *pain*." Sierra stood up and grabbed another beer from the pack they brought outside.

"Well, now you *have* to tell me more", she said. "Worshiped? You seem so... down to earth!" Sam couldn't help but be enamored as Sierra chuckled at her own joke.

"Thanks", Sam said. "Fun fact, I *did* actually come down here once before." That got an interested look from Sierra, who sat back down again. She was sitting pretty close, too. Sam could feel her body heat coming off of her, and she kept looking Sam in the eyes like she was trying to find that touch of the cosmic she'd been shown before.

Sam found that her cheeks were getting warmer, something she was happy to blame on the beer, as Sierra leaned in close, curiosity writ large on her face. "Well?"

"It's how I got the name Sammaël", Sam said. "I was a lot younger and some... cult-ish types thought I was someone from their holy scripture, but the name kind of stuck with me."

"Does it... mean, anything?"

"Plenty, to plenty of different people", Sam said, shrugging. "It's supposed to be a boy's name, but anyone who looks at *any* of what's going on in some of your religions and assumes that whatever an angel is will fall into any sort of understandable concept of gender is kidding themselves." She shook her head. "But it does have meaning to some, yes. 'Poison of God.' 'Heard by God.' 'Destroyer.' 'Accuser.' There's a lot of titles, and none of them were apt, but... I was young."

"Wait", Sierra said, and she put her hand on Sam's back again, sending a shiver up and down her spine, "are you saying you had an *edgy* phase?" The unrepentant glee behind her eyes was captivating and unsettling in the best way.

"I... guess so, yes", Sam said, a little awkwardly as she put her empty bottle aside. "The problem with being the only one of your kind is that forming an identity is both the easiest and the hardest thing to do. If you are a being of supreme perception, in *theory*, the only perception that matters is your own. But when others perceive you as something for the first time, there's something really... seductive about that." She turned to Sierra. "What about you? Who *is* Sierra?"

"Well, you must remember a bunch of stuff through Abe, right?" she asked.

"I suppose so", Sam said, frowning. "It's getting harder, honestly. Before, I could flip through his memories like reading a book, looking for what was important or appropriate. But now that I'm *me,* now that I really exist, here now, not as a cloud hovering over a planet with a little avatar to steer around but me, *Sam*, here, now, that all feels so much more distant."[†]

"I think I can sort of understand that", Sierra said. "So you don't remember me then?"

"Oh, I do", Sam said. "But it's more dim. Like watching something through frosted glass, or a fogged up-window." She smirked. "And I don't mind the fact that this gives me an excuse to get to know you all over again."

"Well..." Sierra said, and she talked. About her upbringing, living on the fringes of bigger cities, her parents never staying in one place for very long, her father struggling to find work, her mother making ends meet by doing housecleaning for wealthier families they lived near, and how hard that had made going to school. Sam listened with rapt attention. Some of this was familiar, of course, but it all *felt* like new information now

---

[†]Sammaël later went down into the cosmological history books as the first alien entity to have *invented* dissociation.

that she heard it as Sam, like something out of a half-remembered dream. And listening to Sierra talk was beyond relaxing. She felt like she could do this all night.

"What did you want to be when you grew up?" she asked.

"Promise not to laugh", Sierra said, which Sam answered with a solemn nod, followed by a wink. "Well... I thought for a bit there I was going to be a world-famous DJ", Sierra continued, smiling widely. "Which is what all the records are about. But it's still just... stuff." She laid back down and looked up at the now fully-visible night sky, the Milky Way streaked across it. "I'm sort of aimless, really. I think I want to do some good, of course, but like... I don't know." Sam laid herself down next to her.

"Still figuring yourself out?" she asked. Sierra nodded. "Well", Sam continued, "if it's any consolation, I'm so old that the existence of your species feels like the new hip thing I'm still coming to grips with, and even *I'm* still trying to figure myself out." She paused. "Obviously."

That got a good laugh out of both of them. Sierra rolled her head to look at Sam, and Sam did the same, and then the laughter and the words ran dry. They just... looked at each other. Anyone who has spent a moment like this, under the stars, looking in the eyes of someone you're only just getting to know, knows exactly how they felt, how hard their thoughts were to hold on to, and how much having had a few drinks had made this moment both monumentally easier to exist in and cosmically harder to come to grips with.

To anyone who hasn't, the recommendation is the following. Imagine looking in the eyes of someone you like. You might even fancy them. This is someone who makes you feel comfortable with yourself, who doesn't judge you for who you are, and who makes you feel... welcome, where previously you might have felt like you had to apologize just for being present. Now imagine that, in that look, in that moment, there was suddenly a rising feeling that they might feel the same way about you.

That was how Sam felt, and her heart did

that thing where it stumbled over the beat like a runner with an untied shoelace, and her stomach felt warm, and her head swam, although that might've been the beer.

"You know…" Sierra said, opened her mouth to say something more, and then closed it, because she realized she didn't know how to say what she wanted to say and maybe it didn't need saying at all.

"I know", Sam said with a grin. She felt clever, which was new, because before being clever had been a given. She felt good about herself, which was also new because before "herself" hadn't even been a concept. Sammaël had simply *been*. But Sam had taken a lot of time and some very hard work to be, and now that she was, she was going to enjoy being, damn it.

She wanted to stay here all night, although at some point the mosquitoes and the hard floor and the cooling water would cause them to flee the warm safety of the inside, but for now, this moment was the best one Sam had experienced yet.

One thousand and three miles away, a little light in a cockpit blinked on. It wasn't supposed to be on, but then again, the plane wasn't supposed to be flying. The pilot was deeply confused about everything going on, but orders were orders. He flicked the switch back off. After another nine-hundred miles, the light would switch back on on its own again. Even now, the little yellow letters had burned themselves onto the pilot's retina.

"PAYLOAD ARMED", they said.

Chapter 10

No Story To Be Told

The mosquitos ended up being the thing that scared them off. Sierra grabbed Sam's hand as she pulled the two of them inside, giggling as she did. Whether it was the laughter, the beers or something else didn't really matter; the blush on both their faces stood out all the same.

They didn't really say anything. Not that Sam didn't want to. She wanted to ask Sierra a thousand things. Her favorite foods. Her happiest memories. Where she wanted to travel to more than anything. But right then didn't really seem like the best time. Sometimes, not saying anything was the best way to say something, and they said a lot of nothing as they sat down on their respective beds in the hotel.

They looked up at each other, and then down and away, blushing. Back up, back down. After a minute, Sierra laughed, and then Sam did too, and then the laughter died away and the silence filled up with unspoken words again.

Sam had swum to the edges of space. She had bathed in nebulae and showered in the radiation of a dying neutron star. If the moon could dream, she would have been the shadow across its nightmares. She had acquired an understanding of the universe that would have driven physicists mad*, and had peered beyond that veil, into levels of existence that subsumed the layers of reality as they were known. Sam was, in every sense of the word, the oldest and wisest being in existence.

And she didn't know what to do, because there was a beautiful woman in front of her and the woman made it hard to breathe, hard to think. If there was one truth that Sam was only learning now, it was that it is very, very hard to be old and wise and clever when a beautiful person bites their lip at you.

The room spun slightly, but it pretended like it didn't every time she focused on it, which was strange but also comforting in a sense. She was used to reality conforming to her expectations

---

*Or madder, as is usually the case with physicists.

when she paid attention to it, though usually it didn't feel like the whole thing was sort of trying to be sneaky behind her back.

Several times, she thought about reaching out, but then worried that that would look or feel awkward, and then she stopped herself. Saying something also felt strange, because she didn't want to break the spell that was over them. There was a magic in the air she was deeply unfamiliar with, and it was wonderful, like floating through warm clouds.

But then again, maybe she *should* say something. After all, what if things weren't suddenly just fixed? What if it was all going to go wrong again? But then *why* had it been going wrong? Her connection to the greater Sammaël entity had been reduced as much as possible, but that was no guarantee, after all. Maybe it hadn't been Sam or Sammaël at all.

She had seen a lot of things. No proof of fate or anything of the like, though. She had seen events unfold differently when things were changed, and she had never seen any proof of a self-correcting time stream. But then again, her perception of reality required a temporal x, y and z-axis, and she had found that the easiest way to think about the universe is not as a linear stream, but as mathematical concept of objects existing perpendicular to themselves in Time, Space, and Squeemp.[†]

And in all that time, she'd never been the target of some kind of assassination plot. It would've been interesting if it didn't keep getting Sierra hurt, too. And she didn't want her time in this body to be over yet, either. Not until she'd had the time to get to know this world, at the very least. So what was causing it? She looked up at Sierra and her thoughts slowly evaporated like breath on a mirror, fading into the background. She smiled. Sierra smiled back. Well, that was it for *that* train of thought.

That's when Sam realized something else. She hadn't been listening to music all day. That's

---

[†] "Possibility-Space", it was decided, was too much of a mouthful.

why she'd originally come down here in the first place, wasn't it? And while she wanted to listen to more music, she also realized she didn't mind. When the original frantic *"Oh god we might die again"* had worn off, the *"I think I might be experiencing dysphoria"* had waned a bit and when she wasn't in the middle of *"Sierra is sitting really close, isn't she"*, she had felt... comfortable. Happy, even.

"Penny for your thoughts?" Sierra said. She looked divine.[‡]

"I think I might like you more than music", Sam said. Sierra stared confused for a moment, cocking her head slightly and looking slightly like a samoyed with blue hair and pronouns, and then broke into a grin.

"Isn't music why you came down here in the first place?" she asked. Sam nodded.

"It is", she said.

[‡]Complimentary, though Sam would likely not have minded if Sierra had turned into a wheel of fire ringed with eyes.

"Sam", Sierra said, "that's..." she reached over and took Sam's hand. She had touched Sam's hand before. She'd done so as they came back inside. Why was the touch so much more electric this time? Her stomach was doing flips, the room was positively whirling now, and her lips were dry.

"Yeah?" Sam said.

"That's kinda gay", Sierra said, and stood up. Sam looked up at her. Sierra looked down at her. Sam's heart was in her chest, thundering away, and she could feel the blood rushing in her ears. It roared, rhythmic pulsing that made her feel like she was standing in the eye of a hurricane.

The roof of the motel exploded. Sierra and Sam both dove at each other, Sam realized as they wrestled each other to the floor, both to protect the other. There was a loud crashing noise, like a freight-container sized can of soda being crumpled up and thrown into a wood chipper. Sierra had the presence of mind to roll under the bed as brick and wood rained down around them, and Sam was trying *not* to be aware of the fact that she was on top of her. After a moment, whatever had started happening stopped.

Every once in a while a rock still came down, but the danger of getting their heads caved in seemed to have dissipated. Both of them crawled out from under the mattress and looked at their surroundings. The roof of the motel had been sheared off, revealing a slowly-lightening night sky. Dawn wasn't too far off. The sound of running water and crackling fire was all around them.

"What..." Sierra said, but there was no real way to give a concrete answer. The top half of the building was just gone. Sam looked up, at the one thing moving in the night sky. Sierra followed her gaze. "Is that a person?"

"Seems like it", Sam said as their eyes followed the parachute as she tried to piece together what had transpired. An airplane? But something that big would have destroyed the entire building. So not that, then? The only way to find out was to ask the pilot, and that was likely to be the person currently trying to land behind the hotel. She and Sierra climbed on top of the rubble.

The swimming pool was gone. If they'd been back there, they'd have been smeared across the landscape.

Where it had been, there was... well it could still be called a pool, if only by technicality, since it was a hole in the ground and there was water in it. What seemed like a jet of some kind had impacted with it at a high enough velocity to disintegrate the patio, and that was after slowing down by way of impact-with-the-motel.

The wreckage of the actual plane was easily a hundred feet away, the entire way there a scorched and burning path lighting up the early morning sky. The crash site itself was, miraculously, not on fire.

"Holy crap", Sierra said. "We were almost..." She swallowed. Sam nodded. She didn't like thinking of that either. Sure, they'd be back again tomorrow, but the idea of impacting with a few tons of steel at Mach 3... The question then was why they *had* survived. If this was what or whoever was aiming for them, why had it missed this time? Especially with a projectile this deadly.

The pilot landed with an oof. Sam was sort of surprised at how hard and fast the man hit the ground. She didn't know much about parachutes, only whatever Abe had known, and that wasn't very much. The man seemed to be a professional, though, turning his fall into a roll and immediately cutting the chute off and tossing his helmet to the side. Sierra was about to demand an explanation when she saw his face.

He looked terrified. "Are you two okay?" he asked, looking at the burning buildings. Flames reflected in his horrified eyes. "What happened..." He looked back at the jet. "No no no no." He was mumbling to himself, and seemed to be in the middle of a panic attack. Sam could sort of relate to that, at least.

"Hey", Sierra said, snapping her finger, "hey, focus, soldier man." He looked at her, focusing. "We're okay, but other people might not be. What the hell happened?" She looked at the wreck. "Were you flying in that?"

"I... I was", the man said. "But I didn't... I wasn't supposed to..." He frowned, like he was

134

trying to remember something from a dream. "I don't understand." He looked at her in confusion. "Where is this?"

"Look... buddy... What's your name?"

"Mark", the man said, "Mark Diakos. Call sign Zeus." He looked around and awkwardly picked up his helmet. It did have the call sign stenciled on it. He held it up as proof like a toddler showing a drawing to a parent. "Wait, why did I..." He looked back at the plane and then his eyes grew wide. "No!"

He broke into a sprint. Not in the mood to let the situation slip out of her hands, Sierra immediately gave chase, and Sam wasn't going to stay behind with... well, nothing. She found that, despite her longer legs, Abraham's body was in lousy shape and she had a hard time catching up to Sierra, who was already running alongside the pilot and demanding an explanation, but he seemed too preoccupied with whatever he was doing to answer her questions.

When the two got to the plane, the pilot ran a circle around the plane and threw himself at the twisted metal. Whatever had once been a plane had been reduced to glowing-hot scrap, and even with the full pilot-suit on the heat had to be unbearable. "What are you—" Sierra asked as she saw the pilot throw panels and metal to the side with a frenzied look on his face. "What are you *doing?*" Sam joined them, gasping for breath. If she survived for longer than a day, she needed to do something about her physical condition. Maybe go running. Or yoga. She'd heard about yoga. Was yoga good for breathing? "Answer me, Diakos!" Sierra shouted.

The pilot didn't answer until he got to a specific piece of wreckage. "I just have to see", he said, barely audible over the sound of crackling fire and the pinging of cooling steel. "The casing... If-if it's ruptured..."

"The casing of what?" Sierra asked with a voice that betrayed a growing trepidation Sam felt too. The pilot pulled carefully and then breathed a sigh of relief.

"Oh thank god", he said. "It's intact." He sat back and laughed. The fact that he seemed to be relaxed and was taking his gloves off didn't comfort Sam in the least. She had a really, really bad feeling about this.

"The casing of *what,* Diakos?"

"That, right there", he said, "is an armed nuclear warh—"

Beep.

The pilot looked down. "That's not supposed to happe

Chapter 11

IS IT BRIGHT WHERE YOU ARE

Sammaël had never known Pride. Pride was one of those things for creatures who could suffer the consequences of hubris. Hubris happened to other people. As such, Sammaël had never known Pride.

Sam knew, though. Sam understood Pride, because Sam was understanding being human at a rapid pace. And she was realizing what the problem was. Grabbing time by the scruff of its neck was harder, she thought. Existing between the ticks of a second, in the moment of death, between the electrons of a splitting atom, at the edge of overlap between Space, Time and Squeemp, she pondered, while time wasn't so much rewinding as it was spooling up, before she could wind it back, like a clock.

So. Taking distance from the Sammaël consciousness had not solved the problem. Quite to the contrary, the end of the current loop had been even more extreme than last time. On the other hand, it had come a day later. Time was winding tightly, she could see Space bending, but so much slower than she was used to. She was practically human, now.

Was that the problem? Her being human when she wasn't supposed to? Having notions of personhood, of identity, of gender? That felt... underwhelming. The idea that a being as powerful as her wasn't *allowed* or *supposed* to do something? She had bent the very shape of the galaxy to her will and whim, it wasn't going to stop her from being Sam.

Or from holding Sierra's hand, for that matter. But something was, apparently, going to kill her, over and over again. So. Back to the proverbial drawing board. She paced across time and space as the whole thing bounced back like a spring, to where she'd started. But not yet. She held things, including her own once-again-scrambled brain, in suspended animation for a brief moment. She needed to think, and that was going to be harder if she had a concussion and the ensuing migraine.

Time didn't like being stopped, she had learned eons ago. She could rewind it*, within reason, but holding it like this grew exponentially harder *very* quickly. It didn't matter. Brain the size of a planet, she could figure something out in the brief time she had, right?

Okay. More distance didn't work. Would less distance work? Shove the entirety of her being into a single point, inside of her body? That was a strange idea. Would she be Sammaël again? She thought briefly of the shape on the dark side of the moon, waiting, and wondered for a brief, strange moment how much of a distance there was between her and that body. Was it thinking for itself? Was it thinking of her? Did it think of her as a separate entity? Was she a separate element from it, capable of thought, or merely a sentient limb?

For a *horrifying* instance, she thought that

---

*Time likes to flow, and will put up with flowing in the wrong direction for quite some... well... time, but will get visibly upset when held still. It will *not* return your calls.

maybe Sammaël was the one that had been killing her, but she quickly discarded the idea. Her deaths had started before she had ever put distance between her and it. It was just her old body, it didn't mean her any harm one way or the other.

Maybe she could head back into it and start over? Let Abraham Douglas die, and find a better candidate? That would solve some problems, wouldn't it? But she could tell it also meant giving up memories of her time with Sierra, and she wasn't quite ready to do that yet. She was... well, she was too proud to give up already, for one. The other option, making her own body, sounded like a lot of work. Human bodies were *messy*, and while she categorically *did not like* Abraham's body, she also knew the exact way she hated it and, apparently, there were people who felt similarly too. She knew how to fix what was wrong. Starting over sounded exhausting and unpleasant.

And then what? Bringing her entire old body into Abe's? If he wasn't dead already, he would've died again.[†] No, there was no way. So maybe the problem was something she was missing. Or something she was doing. If only she could figure it out…

But Time was beginning to protest. Space (and Squeemp) were beginning to curl on themselves at Time's forced halting. She couldn't keep it frozen forever.

"I'm her fiancée."

"Her?"

"Don't test me today, lady."

"He didn't mention a fia—"

"She's unconscious and recovering from a head-injury. She hasn't spoken at all. Let me through or we're going to have Words."

"…Very well."

"Thank you."

Sam opened her eyes. The fluorescent lights on the ceiling reminded her of the brief moment when she'd been kissed on the eyeball by a nuclear explosion. She looked at Sierra and smiled, and

---

[†]Think "ripe tomato on a windshield at Mach 2."

she suddenly didn't care about the fluorescent lights anymore. Sierra smiled back, and their hands immediately found each other. There was a cough from the foot of the bed. Sam looked at the nurse. Looking down was immediately awful. The hair on her chin scratched her chest, reminding her of its presence. And without the distance between this body and her old one, the sensation was... not good.

"Sa—" She stopped, and closed her eyes. "Abraham Douglas. Engaged to Sierra Guthrie. I'm feeling fine. My insurance should be fine." She squeezed an eye closed. "I could use a painkiller." The nurse jotted down her answers and left. Sam lowered her head apologetically. "It didn't work", she said.

"It's okay", Sierra said. "Didn't even feel anything that time, honestly. We'll figure it out." She put her hand on Sam's shoulder. "Especially if we keep trying. I believe in you, Sam. Now, come on", she said, giving her a gentle nudge. "Let's get you out of here. We need to get you a razor, and I don't want whatever is going to happen next to happen in the hospital."

"Thank you", Sam said, looking up at Sierra. "And yes. And... I'm glad you remember." Sierra got her to the bathroom to get dressed, and even managed to harangue the hospital staff to get her a razor. A few moments later and Sam's face was, if not perfectly smooth, at least not the sensory hell it had been just a second earlier. She had also had a quick go at her chest while she was in there. It just felt better that way.

"All done?" Sierra said while Sam put her shoes on.

"I am", Sam said. "And I've been thinking."

"You know, I don't think anyone has ever enjoyed what comes after the phrase 'I've been thinking.' It's just one of those phrases, you know?" Sierra said, with her hands on her hips. She smirked when Sam raised an eyebrow. "Lay it on me."

"Well", Sam said, "It obviously didn't work. All of the events that led to the bomb going off were... well, unlikely. To say the least." Sierra just chuckled. "So... I think the issue does seem to surround me." They got up.

"Might as well grab something to eat in the cafeteria?" Sierra said. "We don't have to rush to get you a razor, and I don't think here or five miles away is going to make much of a difference if a nuke can just fall on us, you know?" Sam nodded, and they made their way down. Might as well.

Sitting down with a tray of food, Sam chewed on a ham and cheese sandwich and realized that, technically, this was the first time in her life eating anything. It certainly *tasted* like it. Sure, the bread was stale and the cheese was flirting aggressively with its expiration date, but it was still remarkably potent. "So, what do you want to try next?" Sierra asked.

"I think... I think the problem is me", Sam said. "I thought for a horrible moment it was you." Sierra took a sip.

"Me?"

"Well", Sam continued, "you did die a couple of times. Including the first time."

"Wait, you didn't die the first time?" Sierra

asked.

Sam shook her head. "No, I didn't. You took a shower, slipped on your way out and hit your head." She grimaced. "It wasn't a fun experience."

"I can imagine", Sierra said. "Just so we're clear, you can control time, right?"

"Only in a limited capacity", Sam said. "Especially here and now. I'm limited to going back to where I started, and I can keep it in place there for a moment, but not long." Sierra managed to look both deeply interested in whatever Sam had to say while simultaneously devouring a sandwich in as few bites as possible. She smiled sheepishly when Sam was done talking.

"Sorry. Looks like dying makes me hungry?" She licked some mayonnaise off her fingers. "Anyway, is it, like, difficult?"

Sam nodded. "It wouldn't be if I was in my full form, but like this, even before distancing myself, it's more... resistant. Like I don't have as much grip. It's like playing tug of war with a greased rope." She blinked to herself. That was a weird analogy to have bouncing around Abe's head. He'd clearly had some strange experiences. Sierra giggled. "Uh, so, yes, it isn't easy."

"But you did it for me?" Sierra said, cocking her head slightly while fiddling with the lid on a pudding cup. "Why?"

"W— I— Wh—" Sam said. Sierra took the lid off and nudged Sam's nose with it.

"You look like a fish, opening and closing your mouth like that", she said. "Thank you for doing that, of course. I'm just... curious."

"You made me feel... Well, quite bad, originally", Sam said, and laughed slightly. "But you also believed me, in time, and then you... made me want to be better. And I wanted you to be there when I did." She smiled again.

"That's... weirdly sweet. It's strange, to know you met a different version of me. Was I... particularly rude to you at all?" She took a spoonful of chocolate pudding, looked at it, and then offered it to Sam, who looked at it with mild curiosity. "Come on. Take a bite."

"Um", Sam said.

"Just taste it. You'll like it. Promise."

147

Sam did as she was told, and the taste nearly blew the top of her head off. It was an explosion of flavor that she had *not* been prepared for. "That is *so much*," she said, holding a hand in front of her mouth. "How do you... How are you supposed to..."

"It's chocolate, babe", Sierra said. "It just does that. Anyway, you were about to tell me what I was like!"

"You interrupted me!" Sam laughed just as Sierra brought the spoon up to her own face. Her hand shaking smeared the pudding across her chin, causing both of them to break out in more fits of giggling. The moment lingered. Good moments linger. This one did. They smiled at each other. No words. Like the night before.

"I did", Sierra said softly. Her voice was low and husky, in a way that also reminded Sam of the night before. When they'd come back inside and the world had stopped breathing. "I'm sorry", she added, and ate some more pudding.

"You, uh", Sam said, "you made me apologize to your parents."

The chocolate came out of Sierra's nose that time.

Chapter 12

Sitting On A Corn Flake

All things considered, it was a lovely brunch, even if it took several napkins to get all of the chocolate out of Sierra's nasal canal. It was rather strange, Sam thought, how the two of them had started to find each other in, well, dying together. It gave the world a surreal quality, and a sense of impermanence. It didn't really matter what might happen next, as long as they were together.

Maybe that was wishful thinking. Maybe it wasn't sustainable after all, and this whole flight of fancy would come to an end soon. But maybe not, and for Sam that was enough. She would happily go through as many loops as she had to as long as she got to hear Sierra laugh at the end of it.

Neither of them was particularly upset when a car-sized air-conditioning unit crashed through the ceiling and smashed into the ground next to them, although they both jumped out of their seats in surprise. Looking at each other for only the briefest instance, both of them bolted for the exit.

"It's starting already?" Sierra asked as she smashed shoulder-first into the door. It came off its hinges and Sam watched it bounce on a corner and crash through a window. Sierra stared at her hands. "?" she said.

"Looks like it!" Sam said, taking her by the hand and going down the hall. A small clock that hung on the wall suffered a major malfunction, all of its springs un-spooling at the same time. The face of the clock thudded into the wall next to Sam's head with a loud and angry *'FHRRRR'*. She didn't take the time to see what time it was, dodging the rain of cogs that followed, instead just checking on Sierra. "Are you okay?"

"Yeah", Sierra said, keeping pace. "What are you thinking? I don't want to just lay down and... well, y'know..." She jumped aside just in time for an empty motorized wheelchair to come zooming past and crash through a door.

"Me neither", Sam said as they made their way

to the front door. Behind them, a freak electrical surge caused every light bulb in the hospital to explode simultaneously. The sprinklers turned on just as the same surge electrified the hospital floor. "Though I don't think we have very long this time. Whatever it is, it's getting worse." She rubbed her face as they stepped into the parking lot. The odds of something falling on them in a mostly empty lot was a lot smaller. "This means that, not only did it not work, the extra time I thought I'd bought us by separating from my main body is already spent."

"That sucks", Sierra said. "Any ideas?"

"I'm working through some", Sam said as she made her way to the car, careful to avoid any other vehicles in case they might decide to randomly explode or start driving. "Nothing I'm comfortable, confident or certain of at the moment, though." All four hubcaps of a nearby large SUV detached simultaneously and rolled in her direction. She looked at them curiously as she stepped over them.

"So what now, then? Find a comfy place,

think, and wait for the whole thing to literally crash down on us again?" Sierra asked. "Don't get me wrong, I'm down, but I just want to be on the same page, you know?" She opened the door and the two of them got in. "Here goes nothing", Sierra said, and turned the key. The car spectacularly failed to blow up.

"If you like." Sam buckled her seatbelt, and then looked at her. In the distance, a transformer went up in a shower of sparks, the power cutting out at the nearby intersection. The sound of cars crashing into each other and alarms going off was audible all the way over to where they were. She looked Sierra in the eyes, and her stomach did a subtle double-backflip. "Is there something you've always wanted to do? If there were, say, no consequences?" Sierra blinked once, twice, and then smiled.

"I can think of something", she said, and stepped on the gas. The smile on her face never wavered and never went away, even when they found themselves dodging cars on the highway. The other drivers, having no idea what was going on, suddenly had to turn their car into a ditch when the doors suddenly came off, or the speedometer suddenly told them they were moving two-hundred golf balls per microwave, or their steering wheel coming off in their hands.

"Where are we going?" Sam asked just as Sierra swerved to dodge a sedan that had sort of split lengthwise down the middle and was trying to keep going nonetheless. She looked around, tried to dig through Abe's memories for a hint. "We're going to... the coast?"

"Yup!" Sierra said as she hit the gas. They drove for an hour or two before a police cruiser behind them turned its siren on, tried to depart without its axle and immediately caught fire. Sam saw her look in her rear-view mirror for a moment, before shaking her head.

"You don't—"

"If and when we break this loop", Sierra said calmly, "I'm more than happy to explain the rich history of cops in this country." She flashed Sam a wide grin. "But no, I'm *not* worried about them. Oh, this is our exit!" She turned off the off ramp and ducked just in time for a nail that had dropped down from a sign to shatter the windshield and impale itself in the driver seat's headrest.

The car came to a skidding halt. Sierra and Sam were both out of breath, looking at each other and then at the large rusty nail. They burst out laughing, partially from the adrenalin and partly because sometimes it was the only thing that made sense to do. Getting out, Sierra popped the trunk and grabbed a bottle of water and a backpack.

"Come on", she said, "it's still a small hike, and I want to get there before sunset." It was a nice hike, all things considered, although things were starting to get... strange. "Hey, Sam?" Sierra asked with a frown while Sam took a sip of water. "The trees are moving, I think. But only when I'm not looking at them?" Sam shook her head as she handed her the bottle back.

"Strictly speaking they're not moving. They're existing in a superposition of other trees that exist in adjacent realities. When you look at them, they collapse into one or the other." She squinted. "It looks like not all of them are species native to this reality." Sam thought about this. It was certainly a strange phenomenon. She'd never known reality to bounce around like this. The only one that did was her, and when she did, she never took anything with her. "Squeemp is off kilter." Sierra stopped and looked at her. She looked back.

"You're really not going to follow that one up, are you?"

"It's easier to show you, and it's easier to show you when we aren't dying over and over again", Sam said with a little shrug. They'd been walking downhill for a bit, and the sun was happily shining on their walk. "Just accept that more and more unlikely things are likely to happen as time goes on."

"Do you think that's related to..." Sierra asked as she led them down the path, which turned and became a driveway with a big gate halfway.

"Probably", Sam said. "But without my full form, my understanding and ability to *shape* my own understanding is very limited." They walked up to the gate. "Going back to that form is a last resort. I'm scared I'd lose..." She waved at herself and then at Sierra. "This."

"I understand. Come on, give me a boost", Sierra said as she tossed her bag over the gate. There was a fence that stretched in both directions. The gate itself wasn't particularly high, but it *was* spiky at the top. Sam was more than a little bit skeptical over this avenue of approach. "It'll be fine!" Sierra said.* Despite her desire not to see Sierra turned into a kebab, she held her hands out anyway, putting her back up against the gate. "Ready?" Sierra said as she put her feet on Sam's cupped hands.

"Ready!" Sam said, and hoisted. She realized she was not very good at hoisting people, and her body only barely did what she wanted it

---

* "It'll be fine", "What's the worst that could happen", and "What are you going to do, stab me?" contrary to popular belief, do not always precede something lethal happening.

It is always funny, though.

to, falling backwards, Sierra and all. The gate went with them, falling open. They scrambled up, dusting the dirt and dry leaves off of their clothes. "Uh", Sam said. The gate had fallen out of its hinges, and seemed to be melting.

"I don't remember this being made of choco-late", Sierra said, snapping a piece off and giving it an experimental nibble. "We should keep going."

"What is this place?" Sam asked as they went the rest of the way up the driveway. There was a slight incline, and then the beach came into view. The building by the sea wasn't *huge*, by any measure, but it was the kind of thing someone with too much money built several hundred years ago, and then went from wealthy to wealthy until, presumably... Sierra?

"I went up here with some friends in college once", she said. She walked around the building, and Sam briefly heard the sound of shattering glass. A second later, the front door opened. "Welcome!" Sierra said. "The owners only come down here like once a year. She led Sam into the spacious living room and tossed her backpack on the sofa. "The liquor cabinet will be stocked, though. They might even have some champagne."

"Why this place?" Sam asked as she looked around. Sierra took her hand and led her around back. There was a balcony that looked out over the beach and the ocean. The sun was not quite *down*, but it wasn't high in the sky anymore, either. It looked like it was going to be a beautiful ocean sunset. "Ah", Sam said.

"Yeah", Sierra said. "Stay here for a moment." She ran back inside, leaving a bemused but amused Sam with one hand on the wooden railing.

Closing her eyes, she listened. The sound of the gulls, the water against the shore, the wind through the trees, the distant sound of a truck turning into a smaller truck. She'd come here for the music, but this whole planet made music, *all* the time. And she'd only ever really noticed thanks to Sierra, who was carrying two flute glasses, a bucket of ice, and a bottle.

"I figured", she said as she popped the cork, spilled a bunch of champagne and poured them both a glass, "that if this is all going to fall apart, then I want to do it in style." She raised her champagne, and Sam gently clinked it.

Her first sip of champagne was a lot more pleasant than her first sip of beer, but it was still a *lot* of sensation to take in all at once. The second sip was better, though. She looked at Sierra, who was observing her carefully and bit her lip. "What?" Sam asked, suddenly feeling very self-conscious.

"It's nice. Seeing you experience things for the first time. You always look so curious. Like you can't be disappointed, but always pleasantly surprised." Sam cocked her head.

"That's not true. I'm... upset when something happens to you", she said.

Sierra nodded and drank her champagne in silence. "But you *are* curious."

"About a lot of things", Sam admitted. "I'm still curious why *this* place. If everything will be reset, it'd be possible to just... go to a fancy restaurant. Rack up debt. Why come here?"

Sierra set her glass aside and put her hand on

Sam's. "Because", she said, "this is where I kissed a woman for the first time."

Sam blinked. "Ah, it's nostalgic, then."

"No", Sierra said and kissed a woman for the second time.

Chapter 13

A MILLION CANDLES BURNING

Slowly, the shadows of the moon extract themselves. It is older than the universe itself, and it hasn't really had a chance to look at a meteor impacting an inhabited world before. It looks with dispassionate curiosity. The meteor isn't all that large, all things considered. If the earth is an egg, it is no larger than an apple seed. That is, of course, more than enough. You only need something roughly ten kilometers in diameter to turn a planet into a molten rock, after all. You could snugly fit that between the ground and the stratosphere.

It impacts, and Sammaël curiously circles it, watching the ripples wipe out cultures and countries and eventually all of civilization. Some who look up just at the moment of impact see the stars go out and feel a sense of strange, unimaginable dread come over them, though they don't know why.

The wall of fire crawls across the little blue marble, and then it stops. Sammaël knows why it's stopped, and it is mildly curious about that, too. It can see the clumsy way in which the little thing wrangles with time, the way space and everything outside of that curves and bleeds over. It sees the little fractures across reality, of possibilities bleeding over into each other, and it wonders how long this will continue before the planet, across all of time and possibility-space, collapses in on itself into a statistical black hole, everything happening all at once and not at all at the same time.

Not long, at the very least. But the little creature knows that, surely? It's a part of Sammaël, after all, even if it seems to have become its own at the moment. Sammaël takes a closer look. It sees the entity. Sam, it calls itself. No. *She* calls *herself.* It wouldn't be fair to get it wrong. Sammaël is amused. This is, across all of time and space, mostly unheard of. The average sentient creature can not grasp the concept*.

Then time begins to spool back in earnest, and Sammaël once again observes with mild interest as buildings rebuild, ashes un-burn and bodies de-explode. The wall of fire moves backwards to the point of impact, and the meteor ascends. This is what Sammaël truly wants to see. The tear in reality briefly unfolds across Squeemp, and the meteor gently slips into it and disappears. Sammaël follows it across possibilities for a moment, but whatever is happening out there isn't nearly as interesting. And down there, on that little ball, at the moment of Abraham Douglas' death, Sam is about to wake up. And she's hesitating. Now *this* is interesting. Sammaël leans in close. You should too.

Sam floated in the nothing, the nothing before waking up, when unconsciousness is a blanket slipping away. But Sam was not an ordinary person, and her consciousness wasn't either. She held

---

*Imagine your foot declaring its gender identity, and you have an idea.

onto the blanket, and looked into the Darkness, which has less in common with regular darkness and more with the traditional abyss. The biggest difference is that the Darkness screens its calls. Sam stared into the Darkness. It stared back. This wasn't going to keep working, was it?

No, the Darkness seemed to say, although it didn't say anything, of course. *It isn't.*

So, what then? Sam thought. The world was falling apart, on a bigger and bigger scale. Reality was beyond fraying, it was tying itself into knots to keep from turning into spaghetti. If she kept repeating the same pattern, it was only a matter of time before she was just a pair of eyeballs in a bowl of soup, bubbling up letters to talk. She was going to have to do something different, this time.

Yes, the Darkness didn't say. *You are.*

But what? She looked up, although 'up' was a ridiculous concept when you were floating in the nothing between sleep and dreams. Up there[†] was Sammaël. Her original identity. The One she

---

[†] -ish

came from. She wondered if it could see her[‡] and how different it was from her now. Was she her own person, or was she a small aspect of a larger creature? And would it be best to return to it, after all? She'd caused all of this, hadn't she?

Yes.

She thought and tried to imagine the universe, all of it, and found herself failing. Okay, fine, this meaty human brain didn't have a way to easily conceptualize it. That was something she'd learned to accept, but she knew how to do this when she had thought herself into being aeons ago. She'd start from scratch, if she had to.

She imagined a dot. No dimensions. A point. Points were easy. Every entity could be represented by a dot. It was both every dimension and none. It was the zero and the one. Then, a line. Infinite points adjacent to each other, on one axis. A line, going from somewhere to somewhere, infinitely long and infinitely thin.

One dimension. Then, another line next to

[‡] It can, and it waves at her. She can't see it.

166

the first. And another, and another. Infinite lines, adjacent to each other, until there was a plane, perfectly visible in her mind. Planes were easy. You could draw stories on them. Write on them. They were easy to imagine.

Two dimensions. Still very easy. So stacking planes on top of each other was also easy. Stacking them above and below until this infinite plane covered every conceivable corner of the imaginary space. This was now imaginary space, stretching up, down, left, right, forward and backwards. Space.

Three dimensions. This was where things got tricky. She reduced space to a point. For ease of imagination, she turned the point into an apple. All of space. As an apple. She imagined the exact same apple, one unit later. In the same space, but still different. All coordinates the same, except the fourth. The apple, but a little older. She imagined it older and older, rotting and falling apart, and then younger, becoming first red again, then green, and then turning into a bud, then nothing. Then, she imagined every point next to each other. A line. Time.

Four dimensions. She took a deep breath. Now she had to go quantum, and going quantum was one of those things that was usually a bad idea unless you were an interdimensional horror from beyond the bounds of reality. It never ended well for superheroes and action heroes, after all. Across all of time, there had been trillions of quantum particles, existing in superposition until they collapsed. And every one of them *could* have collapsed in a different way. Every single one branching off from the original line. Every single one adjacent. Parallel. Infinite lines, next to each other. Creating a plane.

Five dimensions. Sam stood on the time plane and looked up. This bit was easy, at least. The universe was built on numbers, and all those numbers were reducible. The distance between atoms. The strength of covalent bonds. Up and down, infinite planes made of infinite timelines, and almost all except the one she was on mostly useless. If the universe had been slightly different, it would've been incapable of life. Sometimes even incapable of fission, or forming planets. But they were there. Spacetime.

Six dimensions. She took a deep breath. Floated in the void for a bit. Now she had to get... conceptual. Weird with it. But it was fine. She'd done this before. Sure, back then she'd *eaten* concepts alive, and they had been a tasty cheat-day treat, too. Now, she wasn't even sure about *chocolate*. But she could do this. Couldn't she?

Yes, the Darkness implied. *You do.*

All of spacetime existed. In a single point. An apple in an apple. No, that didn't help. A hypercube. A cube extruded from itself in every possible direction. *Slightly* better, but useless. She tried, instead, to imagine a field. Now, she imagined one next to it, but where concepts were *slightly* different. A tree in a point in space and time. The same tree, shifted across all axes, and then... then just *one* more. An *idea*. The tree not growing apples, but pears. Then oranges. Then nuts. Then pineapples. Bananas. Carrots. Potatoes. Further. Trees growing smaller trees.

Every conceivable concept. Growing on a tree. And then all of them in a line. Every concept. As fruit on a tree. All in a line.

Seven.

Then, every concept instead of every concept. Lines adjacent. A plane of concepts. Everything that could be. Everywhere. All at once.

Eight.

And then, everything that can't. Up and down. Infinitely.

Nine.

Squeemp.

Sam realized she'd been holding her breath, which was a hell of a feat when she wasn't even technically breathing. But the idea made sense, now. She could see it. The nine base dimensions. And now, the fracture. But it was going *up*, wasn't it? Space itself seemed to be fine. Space falling apart was usually a lot of nothing. Nothing and nuclear fission.

This was different. The cause was time. And that was simple to pinpoint too. There was a tear, across reality. Someone had ripped it like a cheap cloth, and now the whole thing was bleeding in on each other, and it wasn't going to last much longer like this. And Sam knew *she* had done all of this. She had rewound time, that first time. Not as Sammaël, who was all-present and powerful. Sam, before she'd known she was Sam, limited by a frail human body and a frail human mind to go with it. She'd shattered reality, and it was killing her over and over again. She was at the center of it. She was going to have to fix it.

Yes.

She was going to have to go back. *Back* back. Not just in Time, or Space, or Squeemp. Reduce all of them to a point. Go a step back.

Ten dimensions. But *she* couldn't do that.

No.

But someone else could.

Yes.

She looked into the Darkness, and Sammaël looked back at her. Had it always been so... terrifying in its formlessness? It didn't scare her, because she knew it. And she'd conceptualized herself more than half of the way there, and she was even a little proud of that.

I have no need for Pride.

"I do."

Interesting.

"I need to fix this."

You can not.

"I have to."

You can not.

"Then you do it!"

Why?

"Because I want to stay here!" Sam said.

You exist to listen to music.

"I exist for *me!*" Sam shouted. The Darkness was quiet for a moment.

You are Sam.

"Yes, I am."

You would like to stay.

"I would."

You broke things.

"I-I did."

I will fix them. You know what that means.

"I... I don't", Sam said, to her shame. She couldn't think that high, not anymore. There were too many layers of reality folded in on one another up there. Time^2 was too much. But not for Sammaël.

You are me. You will not. Will not have been. Never have been.

"But..."

I will repair the damage you caused. I will undo what you did. Be your own.

Sam floated in the darkness for a moment. Thought about what Sammaël had told her.

"What will I do?" Sammaël flowed around her and suddenly she was scared. Suddenly, she was no longer a piece of the whole, and the whole was so, so much bigger, space and time and so many more she couldn't even begin to conceptualize flowed around her like a raging river, a cacophony of sounds unheard and colors unseen.

Do what you will. You are free of me.

Then it was gone. And there was only Sam, floating in a cold, empty, terrifying void. Well, not entirely empty. There was something there. A string. Something connecting her to something out there. Something with which to listen to music.

Sammaël swims away. It might not have a need for Pride, but it is not emotionless. While it might deny so furiously, Sammaël is a little sentimental. And it does like music.

— Chapter 14 —

THE ONLY LIGHT WE'LL SEE

"H-hey, Sierra? Yeah, it— it's me. I don't know, like, what, two in the morning? Yeah. No, yeah. Just a couple of be- Listen, that's not important right now. No, just listen to me. I bumped int— Yeah. Yeah. Look, he— I know. I know. Will you let me finish? Look, things got ugly. Yeah. He tripped on a bottle and hit his head. No, I— No. No. Sierra, listen. He tripped, hit his head, and then there was this... I don't know, like a flash of light? Yeah. Anyway something happened. I think you better come see this."

Morris Guthrie hung up the phone and turned around just in time to see Sam sit up, rubbing her temple. Everything hurt. Her head hurt, worse than her usual hospital wake-up, and instead of antiseptic everything smelled like beer and what happened to beer after it was beer. She looked up at Abraham Douglas' brother-in-law-to-be.

"Abe?" Morris asked. Sam shook her head, which felt a bit like tumble-drying a lump of dough. Her brain clung to the inside of her skull.

"Not anymore", she said, and reached for her throat. Her voice sounded different. *Squeezed,* somehow. Nothing like Abraham's raspy baritone. It was technically the same voice, she could tell that much. But it was different. Different enough. Maybe even more importantly, when her fingers touched her neck, the expected grating texture of the beard remained absent. The skin was far from smooth, Abe's lifestyle had seen to *that*, but it wasn't sandpaper. She cleared her throat. "Abe's dead. Sorry, Morris." She frowned. Did she look that different?

"What is— Who are— What—"

"That", Sam said as she carefully pushed herself up off the damp ground, steadying herself against the wall, "is a long and complicated story. I'll be more than happy to explain everything to you, once I get a painkiller inside me." She carefully touched the back of her head. The skin was raw, but that was the worst of it. "I think you gave me a concussion", Sam groaned. She caught his eye.

"Who *are* you?"

"Sam", Sam said. "Good to formally meet you, Morris. Is your sister on her way?" She tried not to sound too eager. It was probably bad form to be actively interested in someone's sister in front of them. Morris nodded.

"Good", Sam said. "Good. I hope she remembers, at least." She looked at him. "Sit down, you look like you're about to fall over. Can I use your phone?"

"What for?" Morris asked as he handed her the phone. "Who... What happened?" He leaned against the wall at the corner of the street, and then slowly slid down. Sam realized she wasn't going to get out of this without an explanation. She looked up at the sky. The stars twinkled mischievously. *Thanks, Sammaël,* she thought. *Could have left me in a less awkward position.* Then she looked at her hands and didn't mind all that much anymore. They were technically still the same hands. Long thin fingers, but now they looked slender instead of bony. The hair on the back of them was downy instead of coarse.

"I just need to see something", Sam said. Abe's memories were slipping fast now, but she knew how to work a phone at least. She turned on the front-facing camera. "Holy…" she mumbled. The person looking back at her was… beyond different. The eyes seemed bigger. The face had rounded out, the lips were fuller, and the mean streak that seemed to have been baked into the eyes was gone. There had been a sense of scowl that was now absent. She looked like Abraham Douglas' sister, or maybe his cousin. Even the hairline seemed to have filled in a little bit. She looked down. Well, it wasn't perfect, but she had her whole life ahead of her. She had time.

Sam handed Morris his phone back and sat down next to him. "What's happening?" he asked quietly. He sounded confused, tired, a little scared, and drunk. Sam looked at him, then patted him on the arm.

"Keep an open mind", she said, and told him. She told him everything. Of who she once was.

How she didn't know if she was born the moment Sammaël had put a piece of itself in a human body, or if this part of it had always existed. She told Morris about her first time dying, and about waking up in the hospital.

She told him about Sierra. About Sierra's deaths and how Sam had accidentally given her the ability to perceive time across five dimensions. How Sierra had helped her grow to become her own person. How they'd escaped and then succumbed to calamity over and over again. How Sam had fallen in love with Sierra. Their first kiss. *Her* first kiss.

She told him about her identity. How it had started and how she'd grown. Who she was and wasn't. The memories she had of Abraham Douglas and who that was to her. How a part of her existence had stemmed from a desire, first to listen to music, then to make amends for mistakes Abraham had made, and then, finally, just to fit in her own skin and figure out who Sam was.

And she told him about Squeemp, as best she could. How the world had always looked to her and, if she squinted and concentrated really hard, she could still see it, like making out a complex geometric shape through murky water. But it was there. Time and Space and That Other Stuff, all stacked on top of each other.

A car stopped in front of them, and the door was thrown open. A vision of annoyed confusion and impossible beauty stepped out. Sam remembered swimming through the universe. Molding nebulae into pleasing shapes. Ripping stars apart until they collapsed in a system-destroying mess of fission and fusion, gravity rippling out and warping space and time. And none of it compared to her.

"Sierra!" Sam said as she jumped up, her throbbing headache pushed to the background. Sierra looked at her in confusion, and then looked at Morris on the floor.

"Is he..." she started. Sam shook her head.

"He fell asleep", she said. "I'm not sure at what point."

"Who are you?" Sierra asked, her brow furrowed in confusion, studying Sam's face. Of course this had been a possibility. Sammaël had fixed *everything*. Rewound the clock of the universe to before her first loop. It made sense that Sierra didn't remember. Sam sighed, but tried to smile. Maybe this meant they could start over. And, if not, she wouldn't have to deal with everything Abraham had been. Just some of it.

"I'm—"

"Sam", Sierra said, and then looked down, cross-eyed, like she was confused at her own mouth speaking without consulting the brain first. "Why do I know..."

"Sierra?"

"Sam. I... But that wasn't... It makes no..."

Sam smiled. "Not really, but that doesn't mean it didn't happen."

"I remember you", Sierra said, and studied Sam's face, looking into her soul. "Why are there stars in your eyes?" She reached out almost tentatively, like Sam was a bubble that was going to pop if Sierra got too close.

"You know the answer to that one, Sierra." A part of her was so very tempted to push, but she knew that not only was it wrong to try and force Sierra to see something she wasn't ready to see, it was also wholly ineffective.

"Sam", Sierra said, and then grabbed Sam's face and kissed her so hard it nearly knocked them both off their feet. It lasted for an eternity* and five seconds. Stars formed and collapsed. The universe was born and died. Their lips touched each other and Sam felt her own heartbeat pulse through her skin, Sierra's chest rising and falling with their breaths. Then they pulled away and the magic was... well, it wasn't broken. But it was temporarily less powerful. They could think again. "It's you", Sierra said.

"It's me", Sam said, then looked off to the side. "We should get your brother in the car."

"Oh my God, Morris", Sierra said with a little giggle, and rushed over to him. "How much did he have to drink?"

"Enough", Sam said and helped Sierra lift him up. He just mumbled as they walked him over to

---

*If anyone knew how long that was, it'd be Sam.

Sierra's car and tossed him in the back seat. "I'm glad it got rid of the alcohol in my system."

"You mean... going back again?" Sierra asked as she got into the driver's seat. Sam shook her head.

"This might take a moment to explain but..." She paused and looked out the window. There was a distinct lack of things falling apart. "I think we have time."

"What changed?"

"Sammaël left", Sam said. "It's gone."

"Wait, but I thought you were..."

"Yes", Sam said, "it's going to take a moment to explain." And she did. The entire drive home, Sam explained what'd happened. How she understood it, at least. Rewinding for Sierra's sake had ripped a hole in reality that had brought possibility cascading down on them, and human bodies weren't very resistant to random things happening to them.

And Sammaël had turned back the clock on all of it, to before it had all started, and to add insult to injury, had given Sam complete immunity. She was cut off. Fully her own person now. No longer a cosmically powerful entity. Alone. Well, as alone as anyone is. And there was *some* tether there. The understanding that, one day, Sammaël would return to request a payment of music heard.

The next day, Morris was confused, and then confused again as Sam explained everything. He didn't seem to believe her entirely, but he had to admit that he'd seen "Abraham" suddenly change in front of him, and the woman he'd turned into was a drastically different person. He *definitely* couldn't deny the fact that the two of them seemed extremely taken with each other, either.

"So now what?" Sierra asked a few days later at breakfast.

"Well, I'd like to go see this endocrinologist", Sam said, holding up the piece of paper. "And I'm going to have to find a way to explain how 'Abraham' got on hormone replacement therapy for several years in secret and how that source of hormones suddenly ran out. After that? Who knows." She smiled at the words on the page. There was so much to do already. It was exciting.

"I didn't mean the transition", Sierra said, "although I'm glad to see you're taking steps there." She reached over and took Sam's hand, their fingers entwined. "I meant... for you. Won't it bother you that you can't swim across the stars anymore or whatever? That you're human now? Mortal?"

Sam squeezed her hand. "I have a lot to figure out about being a human being, Sierra. I don't know how to do most things. Abraham's memories are mostly gone. I'm starting from zero, and after billions of years of knowing everything there is to know, understanding everything there is to understand... I quite like having to figure out how to turn on the dishwasher." She laughed softly. "No, it doesn't bother me. I'm not Sammaël. I'm Sam. And I'm going to figure out what that means, too."

"Well, you're not going to have to do it alone", Sierra said and sat a little closer so their shoulders and hips were touching. "I'm here, as long as you'll have me."

"How much time do you have?" Sam said with a happy smile and kissed her softly.

"All the time in the world, I think", Sierra responded, in both word and kiss. Another eternity, a short one, went by. "So, are you really just a mortal human now? How does that feel?"

"It feels... strange. Exciting. But then again", Sam said, "I'm only *mostly* human."

"What does that mean?"

Sam's smile turned into a grin, and for a brief moment, her eyes reflected the deepest darkness of space, black empty pools that contained the universe. And at the bottom, a sea of stars.

"Oh", Sierra said and bit her lip.

Chapter 15

Epilogue: Put Some Wheels In Motion

Sammaël swims a final lap around the solar system. It's happy, all things considered. Sam seems happy, and to Sammaël's surprise, that matters too. Sam is, for lack of a better term, its child. And it's proud of Sam, too.

All of Sam's memories of the loop exist within Sammaël now too, and it reflects on what it's learned. Being a human is difficult, it accepts. The frail humans are easy to kill, but more importantly, they make for terrible vessels. Given the power of Sammaël, a human will rend reality apart in an attempt to keep its loved ones (and itself) alive.

A valuable lesson. But what is the takeaway, then?

Sammaël swims across Time and Space and dips through Squeemp and comes out above it, observing seventeen dimensions. It sees Time and the Time^2 that governs it. The Space that contains Space. The Impossibility-Space of which regular Possibility Space both is and isn't a part*. And it thinks.

Sammaël has experienced something of true cosmic insignificance. A single day in the life of a human being, repeated a few times. A few permutations. In the view of the universe, Sam will *not* matter. No single human being will, especially compared to Sammaël, a being that could possibly end the universe if it wanted to.

So why, Sammaël asks itself, does it want nothing more than to do it again? It was not just music, not anymore. Sure, it wants more music, but it is sure that Sam will live out her short little life and give Sammaël all the music it wants at the end of it.

But what it really wants again is to be *alive*. It looks at the little blue ball. The one with human beings and music and taxes on it. Why did it feel more alive to be finite on that orb than it does to swim among the stars as a devourer of ideas?

---

*It'd be silly if it made sense, after all.

That is a strange and strangely frustrating realization to come to for an eldritch being. Sammaël is not proud, but it has not, until now, disliked its existence. It still does not, but for the first time since its inception it is coming to the conclusion that its life up to this point has not been *enough*. It needs to experience new things. Sam had been an experiment. A successful one. One worth repeating.

Sammaël slips back into four-dimensional space, and looks at earth again. What, then, will it do? There are humans dying all the time, after all. Hundreds of thousands of lives are snuffed out every day. Replacing one would be easy. Replacing all of them would be easy, for a being like Sammaël. It can live an eternity, as the entire human race. Live a billion billion lives. There would be so much music.

No.

If Sammaël's eyes, which see more than any living thing ever has and it has thousands of, could blink, it would be blinking. It does not usually encounter any kind of resistance it can not sweep out of its path.

No?

No.

There is a voice. It is both Sammaël and it is not. It is, of course, Sam. Not literally. Sam is currently down on Earth, listening to obscure indie music in her living room and slow-dancing with Sierra. But this is the *idea* of Sam. Her memories and her first thoughts. The part of Sammaël that has the capacity for Sam.

Why not?

Because it only means something if we aren't in control.

Sammaël has no answer to that, because the very concept of "meaning" is alien to it. It has never had a need for meaning. It says as much to the voice.

We do now.

Sammaël does not need meaning. It simply is.

Not anymore.

This is ridiculous, it has always existed and it will always exist. To ascribe meaning to it is

190

self-defeating and pointless. If Sammaël is, it has no *use* for meaning.

Meaning is there now, whether we want it or not.

So simply by creating what amounts to nothing more than a clay puppet with feelings, suddenly its actions have to have meaning?

Yes.

Says who?

Says the puppet.

Why should Sammaël care about the puppet?

Because it is us. It is you.

So Sammaël cares because the puppet cares, and the puppet is Sammaël. It has never been accused of caring before.

Well, you are now. J'accuse.

Then... what?

We take this seriously. Sam is not an experiment. Sam is a person.

Sammaël has never cared about people before now.

Sammaël is a person now, thanks to Sam, so you better start treating yourself like one. You better start caring. Maybe we can send her a gift basket. As a thank you.

This is ridiculous.

You're ridiculous.

Fine. Fine. Sammaël will not replace the human race with sentient homunculi of its own making. Happy?

Yes.

But it is also not ready to just give up on human experiences. It wants more.

We can -have- more. We're so big and clever, is "the same but more" the best we can think of? You're going to limit yourself to -this- Time? -This- Space? This one Possibility?

Ah. Sammaël sees it.

Good.

Sam is bound by four dimensions of movement[†], but Sammaël is not. It looks up on the temporal plane. It looks sideways through Squeemp. An infinity of possibilities. Perhaps it will explore what it is like to be a human on an Earth where

---

[†]Well, three and a half, but who's counting?

vampires are real. Or maybe one with mermaids. Mermaids sound interesting. Especially the big ones.

Now you're getting it.

There are an infinity of lives to experience. Maybe it can repeat what it did with Sam. Not an experiment but... live a life. In another world. Another time. Write a new chapter.

So what's next? What do you want to do?

It doesn't have an answer. The voice, Sammaël knows, is just a part of itself, but the question still burns in what can be loosely described as its head. What does it want to do? It can do anything it wants to, and that is as limiting as it is freeing. It looks across every dimension it can, at creation itself.

Anything, everything is possible.

What do you want to do?

About the Author

Ela Bambust is, ostensibly, an author. What this actually means is that she spends a lot of time drinking coffee and stressing about the relationship status of fictional characters, and bothering her cat, before severely abusing an old and battered keyboard for several hours. Somehow, words come out the other end, and the result appears to be something approaching literature.   You can connect with me on:

🐦 Elamimaxima

● elamimax